At the Olsons'

Dinner was on the table when he got inside. He hardly noticed the smell of burnt rolls and scorched fat from the fried pork chops. He was too hungry even to taste the food. He just shoveled it in, barely stopping to chew before he swallowed. His stomach seemed like a bottomless pit. But finally, after two or three helpings, it felt full, and he pushed his plate away and sat back.

Mr. Olson was chewing noisily, his arms resting on the table, his utensils raised, ready to attack his meat again once his mouth was empty. Mrs. Olson had one hand in her lap and was staring at her plate. No one spoke. No one ever spoke at the Olsons' table. It was so different from his mother's table, where there had always been discussion of the day's events and laughter and storytelling. And where the rolls were never blackened on the bottom.

~

"Buchanan's characters are her strength—well-drawn, believable individuals who do their best to deal with the hand life has dealt them. . . . [This is] a good choice for fans of orphan train stories and for history buffs."   —*Booklist*

~

Jane Buchanan is also the author of *Gratefully Yours* (Puffin), which has been nominated for seven state reading awards. She works at the public library in Meadville, Pennsylvania, where she lives with her husband and their two teenage sons.

Visit her Web site at **www.janebuchanan.com**

Hank's Story

JANE BUCHANAN

SCHOLASTIC INC.

New York Toronto London Auckland Sydney
Mexico City New Delhi Hong Kong Buenos Aires

ISBN 0-439-52041-X

12 11 10 9 8 7 6 5 4 3 2 1   3 4 5 6 7 8/0

Printed in the U.S.A.   40

First Scholastic printing, February 2003

For all the readers who asked

Author's Note

Between 1854 and 1929, more than 150,000 orphaned and abandoned city children rode the Orphan Trains to new lives. They were put on the trains in New York and Boston and transported to rural communities in the Midwest and elsewhere, where they were "placed out" in adoptive and foster homes.

The Orphan Train movement was started in New York City by the Reverend Charles Loring Brace, founder of the Children's Aid Society, in an attempt to deal with the city's growing population of homeless children. While a large number of those who boarded the trains acknowledged that their lives were bettered, others resented the program that placed them in uncaring and even abusive homes.

Thanks to Mary Ellen Johnson, president of the Orphan Train Heritage Society of America in Springdale, Arkansas, for help with research. Thanks also to Muriel Dubois for her encouragement and support; Sally Wilkins for her farming knowledge, and my parents, Nancy and Bill Buchanan, for their birding expertise. Many thanks also to my editor, Beverly Reingold.

Hank's Story

1

Hank Donohue pulled the covers up to his chin and shivered. The animals needed tending—he knew he should get out of bed. But it was still dark outside, and the early autumn chill had gone clear to his bones.

When they first came to Nebraska—he and his brother, Peter, and the twenty-three other orphans from the home in New York—he had looked forward to the mornings. It was late summer, 1923. Hank and Peter had been placed out with Mr. and Mrs. Olson, a childless couple who lived on a farm outside of town. Mr. Olson hadn't wanted to take the both of them, but Peter had told him he wouldn't leave his brother, and finally Mr. Olson had agreed.

But a lot had changed since then. Mr. Olson had turned out to be a drinker and had started in beating Peter for no reason—or for any reason at all. Peter had run off in the night without so much as a goodbye, and Mr. Olson had lit into Hank in Peter's place.

Hank hardly ever had time of a morning to sit by the barn with his pencil and the sketchbook he'd put together with string and paper he'd snuck from Mr. Olson's desk. He was too busy doing chores—his own and now Peter's—to stand and watch the woman who passed down the road at the edge of the pasture, carrying a covered basket and wielding a tall walking stick. Still, he noticed her, and he wondered who she was and where she was going. When he asked about her, Mrs. Olson told him to mind his own business; the woman was crazy, and he'd do well to stay away from her. But there was something about her—the way she walked, her head held high and one ear cocked. She was looking for something, Hank thought. But what?

Hank heard the rooster begin its morning complaint. If he didn't get up and start his chores, he'd have the back of Mr. Olson's hand to answer to. He pushed aside the thin woven blanket and stood up. The floorboards seemed to draw out what little warmth was left in his feet. He went to the washbasin and splashed some cold water on his face. He ran wet fingers through tangled black curls and patted them down with his hands. No need to change. He had worn all his clothes to bed in an attempt to stay warm. He pulled on his shoes and headed out to the barn, grabbing his hat and coat and chucking a hunk of coal into the stove in the kitchen on his way through. He was careful not to clang the stove door or let the back door slam. No sense starting Mrs. Olson on a rampage so early in the morning.

The air felt warmer outside than it had in his room, but still Hank could see his breath in the light from the sun, which was just making its way above the horizon. On the porch he turned up his collar against the wind and grabbed the slop bucket, which held yesterday's scraps for the hogs.

The animals were awake and waiting for him. He dumped the slop in the trough for the pigs. "Better you than me, pigs," he said. "I couldn't eat it when it was fresh."

In the henhouse, the chickens were making a racket. Hank scattered some corn on the ground for them and collected their eggs while they were off eating.

When all the nests were empty, Hank headed back to the barn. He filled the grain buckets for the horses, then braced himself for his least-favorite chore: the milking. The cow looked at him with her sad brown eyes. She lowed and swung her head from side to side. Hank took the pitchfork and scooped up a couple of forkfuls of fresh hay for her to chew on while he milked. Then he got down the milking pail and stool and sat beside her.

Peter had been the one to do the milking. The cow had liked him; he was a natural. Hank felt funny grabbing hold of the cow's udders. It seemed rude somehow. Too personal. He supposed the cow could tell he was nervous. That was what Peter had said, anyhow. "Cows ain't modest," he'd told Hank. "They don't get embarrassed. Giving milk is what they do." He'd showed Hank how to grab the teats and how to squeeze from the top, pushing up, then tugging down until the milk started flowing. So it wasn't that Hank didn't know how to milk a cow; he just didn't like it.

"Okay, cow," he said, placing the milk pail on the concrete floor under her. The cow turned her head to look at him. She blinked slowly, then she lifted her left rear leg and thrust it backward, kicking over the pail. It clanged on the floor and rolled from side to side with a rattle. Hank sighed. Here we go again, he thought. He reached up and patted the cow on the rump. "There, there," he said. "Good cow." The cow snorted and gathered some more hay with her tongue. He supposed she could tell he didn't really mean it.

"Good girl," he said, trying to sound more sincere as he readied the pail again. "You just keep eating."

The cow lowed again. Hank began pulling on her teats. After a while, milk started to dribble, then shoot into the pail. The pail was half-full before the cow decided to kick it again. The hot milk ran out in every direction, in steaming white rivers held up here and there by dams of hay.

Hank bit his tongue. His mother had not allowed swearing. His brother had picked up the habit when they were living on the street, but Hank thought he'd never heard so much as he'd heard from Mr. Olson in the short time he'd been in Nebraska. It would be a better life, the people at the children's home had told him before they put him on the train. He would have a chance to grow up healthy and strong, away from the crime and filth of the city. Well, he had to admit he was stronger than he'd ever been, with all the farm work he did, but he wasn't sure he was any healthier. Between the Olsons' bad tempers and Mrs. Olson's cooking, he sometimes thought he'd have been better off on the street.

2

Hank was eight when his parents died, one after the other, of TB. Peter was ten. His mother had worried about what would become of them. There were no relatives in America, and she had heard bad things about the homes for orphaned children. She had written to her mother and her sisters back home in Ireland, but no one there could afford to send for them. And she didn't know anyone who could feed two growing boys. She had died knowing her children would be alone. She had made Peter promise to take care of his brother. And Peter had—until now.

When they were living on the streets in those two years after their parents died, before they were put in the children's home, they had run into hoboes with grand tales about their adventures riding the rails. After they came to

Nebraska two years later, and the beatings started, Peter talked a lot about running off, taking up the hobo life. Hank thought it was just talk. He knew Peter was hurting—Mr. Olson's beatings were fierce—but Hank didn't think his brother would really leave him there alone.

Peter's talk had brought Hank to tears. "Aw, dry up," Peter had said. "Heck, with me gone, they'd treat you like a prince, I bet you."

Mr. Olson, though, had been furious when Peter came up missing. Hank had thought the old man would be glad, but he wasn't. He had raged and stormed about the house.

"That no-good stinking kid!" Mr. Olson had hollered. "Where's the gratitude, eh? I give him a home, feed him, put clothes on his back, and what do I get?" He had spent hours out searching, but Peter had plain disappeared.

Then Mr. Olson had turned on Hank. "Where'd he go?" he shouted. And when Hank didn't answer him—couldn't answer him; he didn't know—Mr. Olson raised his hand and brought it down hard against Hank's cheek. Hank fell back, partly from the force of it and partly from the shock. What did I do? he wanted to ask, but he didn't. He just looked at his feet and shook his head.

Hank righted the pail again. "Blasted old cow, anyway," he said under his breath. Then he looked around to make sure no one had heard him. A lamp was glowing in the kitchen window. They would be waiting for the eggs and milk for breakfast. He grabbed the cow's udders roughly and began again. This time the cow stayed still, and Hank got nearly a full pail.

He carried the eggs and the milk into the house. Mrs. Olson was sitting at the kitchen table, looking as though she'd just drunk a jar of vinegar. Her hair was tied all over with bits of rags to make it curl. The smell of slightly rancid fat filled the air, and smoke was coming from a grimy iron frying pan on the stove.

"About time you got done," Mrs. Olson barked.

Hank nodded. He had learned not to answer back. He wanted to say, "If your dang cow would learn to stand still, I'd take half as long," but he kept quiet.

"Put the eggs on the table," she said, "and strain the milk. There's dirt all over the pail again." She shook her head, and Hank could hear her mutter, "Don't know why you can't learn to milk a cow. Never had dirt all over the pail when your brother did the milking."

It was almost funny, Hank thought, how Peter could do no wrong now that he was gone. It's my turn to be the bum.

"What are you smiling at, boy?" Mr. Olson had come into the room. His mop of dirty brown hair stuck out in all directions, and his beard was three days old.

Hank lowered his eyes and shrugged. If he said, "Nothing," he would be accused of lying, but if he told the truth, he'd be scolded for having a smart mouth. He braced himself for the back of Mr. Olson's hand. It didn't come. He dared to look up.

Mr. Olson was peering out the window. "Looks like rain," he said. If there was one thing that could distract him from a beating, it was weather.

"You've said that every morning for the last three months," Mrs. Olson said. Her voice was edged with disgust. Hank imagined that if they were out of doors, she would have spit in the dust. "It's not going to rain. This farm is going to dry up and die, and better for it. Maybe then you'll listen to me and move us away from this godforsaken place."

Hank stood at the sink and poured the milk through the sieve. Bits of dirt and straw caught in the wire mesh. He was careful not to spill; Mrs. Olson did not tolerate waste. It occurred to him that he hadn't sprinkled fresh straw over the milk on the floor in the barn. Mr. Olson would be sure to see it when he went out to hitch up the horses. I'll catch it for certain, he thought grimly.

He carried the sieve and the pail out to the water pump on the porch to rinse them. Mrs. Olson didn't have much use for soap or hot water. He took hold of the handle and pumped to prime it. The rusty metal squeaked, and the water began to sputter and then to gush. Hank could feel the water soaking in through the holes in his shoes. It was cold, and his toes ached.

Mrs. Olson came to the door and rapped on the glass. "You think you can let that water run all over the porch? Don't you know there's a drought on?"

Hank stopped the pump. He picked up the pail and carried it back to the barn. The cow eyed him suspiciously.

"Don't worry," he said, "I'm not going to bother you."

She mooed as though to say, "You'd better not." Hank sidled past her and hung the pail on the hook on the wall. As he started back, he remembered about the spilled milk. He could at least cover it before Mr. Olson saw it. Most of it had been absorbed into the concrete, but it was wet, and the cream had clotted here and there in greasy pools. He grabbed some hay from the manger and spread it carefully over the spill. If he'd had more time, he might have scrubbed the floor down, but he didn't think Mrs. Olson would want him wasting precious water on the barn floor.

He had just finished spreading the hay when he heard footsteps behind him.

"What are you doing now, boy?"

Hank stiffened. He was trapped. There was nothing he could say to satisfy Mr. Olson, so he stayed silent and let the movement of his shoulders up and down be his answer. This time Mr. Olson was not distracted by the weather. Hank felt the force of the farmer's fist on his left ear. He fell onto the floor, scraping his knuckles. The startled cow hauled off with her hind foot and kicked him in the shoulder.

"Don't let it happen again," Mr. Olson hollered. "You

think we got food to waste? You'll be eating half rations until you learn to milk a cow without spilling half of what she gives." He turned and stomped off to where the horses were waiting to be hitched up to the plow.

Hank sat up. His ear was throbbing, and his shoulder felt as though it were on fire. He put his scraped knuckle to his mouth and sucked the blood.

"I hate you," he said, spitting in Mr. Olson's direction when he was sure the old man could not hear him. He sucked his knuckles again. He thought about Peter. Peter, who was supposed to take care of him, who had promised their mother on her deathbed.

"I hate you, too," he said. A low train whistle in the distance was the only reply. It was the loneliest sound Hank had ever heard.

3

Hank went up to his room and splashed more water on his face. In the small looking glass over the basin, he could see his ear was swollen and red. His shoulder was stiff where the cow had kicked him, and a deep purple bruise was already forming.

He pulled his hair over his ear. He would say the cow had kicked him, if anyone asked. It wouldn't be a lie, really, he told himself. But he knew no one would ask, except maybe Emily. No one else at the school liked him much.

Emily, who had been placed out the same time he had, tried to be friendly, but she was so busy minding the family's young ones that she didn't have time for much else. The mother, Mrs. Dewhurst, was a real taskmaster. At the home, Emily had shared a bed with Hattie, but Hank had always felt shy around Hattie and got tongue-tied whenever he tried to talk to her. Besides, she hadn't been to school since they got to Nebraska. He saw her in church, but only from across the sanctuary. He didn't have the nerve to talk to her. Anyway, the Olsons and the Jansens, who had taken Hattie in, didn't have much use for each other. Though from what Hank could tell, Mr. Jansen was a kindly man. He always had a smile for Hank, and his eyes held Hank in their gaze when they saw each other at church. Hank was glad Hattie had been placed out with someone like that, rather than a couple like the Olsons, even if Mrs. Jansen did look pretty cold sometimes.

Hank didn't feel like sitting down to breakfast. He wasn't sure he could stomach Mrs. Olson's cooking this morning. He packed up his books and slipped out the back door.

It had warmed up a lot. Good thing, too, because his shoes had gotten so wet that he had taken them off in his room. There was so little left to them, they didn't do much to keep his feet warm, anyway.

Disappointment Creek School was about two miles from the Olsons'. Hank didn't mind the walk. It was quiet, except for the occasional auto or buggy. The birds were plentiful, and he enjoyed trying to figure out which was which. There had been a book at the home with detailed drawings of every bird imaginable. Hank didn't remember all the names, so he made up his own. There weren't a lot of different birds in the city—pigeons, mostly. You didn't need a book to tell you what those were. But here in Nebraska, there were black-eyed red birds; orange-bellied blue birds; yellow darters. Once, in the cow pond near the lower pasture, an assortment of ducks had landed and stayed for a couple of days before flying off toward the south. There had been big white-headed ones, and others with long pointy bills. Still others were all the colors of the rainbow. Those Hank had named patchwork ducks. Mr. Olson had gone out with his gun to shoot some for supper, but he'd missed with the first shot, and the ducks had flown off. Hank had been sorry to see them go, but glad they hadn't been killed. He hated to think of such handsome birds being butchered by Mrs. Olson and fried in that filthy old frying pan that made everything taste rotten.

There were a few other farms on the way to school, and Hank could see a gang of kids walking up ahead, talking and laughing. They each carried a lunch pail. All were barefoot, as he was. He wished he had someone to walk to school with. It made him miss Peter. At least when his brother was here, he'd had someone to talk to. Peter had helped him with his lessons and listened to him gripe about Matthew, the red-haired bully who tormented him on the playground. Peter had even beat Matthew up once. But then he'd been sent home with a note for Mr. Olson, who had clobbered him pretty bad—to show him, he'd said, that you can't just go around beating people up like that.

Hank sighed and shifted his books to his other hand. His stomach was beginning to growl. He was sorry he hadn't eaten breakfast, and he hadn't brought his lunch pail. It was going to be a long day.

He was about halfway to school when he heard the rattle of a bicycle chain behind him, then the sound of rubber tires skidding on the dirt road. He didn't turn around, even when he felt dirt and stones spitting up and hitting his ankles. It was Matthew's idea of a joke. He would put on the brakes and twist the handlebars sideways so that his bicycle came to a sliding stop inches from Hank's heels. What Hank didn't understand was why Matthew never got tired of the trick. But he didn't, especially now that Peter was gone, because he didn't think Hank would do anything. And Hank supposed he was right.

Hank knew the boys at school thought he was a sissy because he drew pictures. It wasn't that he let on about the drawing, but Matthew had stolen his sketchbook one day and shown it around before throwing it in the hole in the outhouse.

That was the day Peter had let Matthew have it. "Why do you let them get away with it?" he'd asked Hank afterward. "Why won't you stand up for yourself? You think I'm going to be around to protect you forever? And why do you have to draw those stupid pictures anyway?"

Hank had shrugged. He didn't know why he let Matthew get away with it. Maybe it was because his mother hadn't approved of fighting.

Peter had apologized later for calling his pictures stupid, but Hank could tell he didn't really mean it. He did think they were stupid, even if he was sorry he'd said so. Still, he helped Hank sneak some paper out of Mr. Olson's desk to make a new sketchbook.

"It's the poor little orphan boy," Matthew said, and he turned to his friends, who had stopped their bikes behind his, and laughed. The other boys laughed, too. Hank always wondered why children thought it was funny that he was an orphan, that his mother and father had died. Even before he'd come to Nebraska, he and the rest of the kids from the children's home had been the object of jokes and laughter. Now he just shrugged and kept on walking.

"Hey!" Matthew called after him. "I'm talking to you!" He dropped his bike with a clatter and ran after Hank, planting himself in Hank's path. Hank stepped to the left. Matthew stepped in front of him. Hank stopped and looked at the red-haired boy. Matthew was about the same size as he was, really, but he sounded bigger. His eyes were always at a squint, and they were rimmed with a yellow crust. Freckles dotted his cheeks and nose. Hank could see where some of the dots ran together like spots of ink on a page.

"Where you going?" Matthew said. He raised his hand and shoved Hank hard on the shoulder.

Hank winced. It was the same shoulder the cow had kicked. There was no sense answering back—it would only give Matthew ammunition to use against him—so he stood there.

Matthew's friends were getting restless. Not enough of a show, Hank supposed. "Come on, Matt," one said. "Let's get out of here."

"Yeah," said another. "We're gonna be late. Mr. Givens'll tan our hides."

"Aw, all right," Matthew said, disgusted. He gave Hank one last shove, knocking his books to the ground. "You were lucky this time, orphan," he said, giving the books a kick. He picked up his bike, swung his leg over the seat, and sped off toward school with his gang behind him.

4

Hank bent down to pick up his books. Mr. Givens would not be happy that they were covered with dust and grit. One of the pages of his reader was torn clear out. It was the page about how boys should play nicely together. That almost made Hank laugh. He tucked the page back in and wiped the books on his pant leg. Then he balanced the stack in his good arm and began walking again.

He would surely be late, and the boys had been right, Mr. Givens would tan his hide. He thought about skipping school altogether. Mr. Givens seemed to delight in humiliating him before the class. Already he had put Hank with the six-year-olds after he had failed his tests—not because he couldn't do the work, but because he had no time now that he was doing Peter's chores as well as his own. He was too tired at the end of the day to take out his books and study.

Besides, what was education going to do for him here on this Nebraska farm? Mr. Givens would ask Hank questions from lessons he hadn't done, and to cipher on the board problems that he hadn't yet learned. And when he couldn't answer, Hank would hear Matthew and the others laughing behind him—especially since Peter wasn't there to glare at them.

Peter. Maybe he'd had the right idea, Hank thought. Maybe he should just run off. He could catch the next train out of Nebraska. He could go to New York and find his brother. But he wouldn't have any idea how to catch a moving train, or where to go once he did catch it. Anyway, Peter would be back for him. He had to stay so his brother would know where to find him. In the meantime, he needed to get to school, and he'd better hurry.

He began to run, but got a stitch in his side before he had gone far and was forced to stop. He was bent over, his free hand on his knee, trying to catch his breath, when he saw movement in the brush by the side of the road. For a moment he thought it was Matthew again, hiding and waiting to ambush him. He stood stock-still and watched. Out of the brush came a bird as big as one of the Olsons' chickens. It was speckled brown and white with bright yellow bars over each eye, like eyebrows. Its pointed tail was bent straight up behind it. One wing was dragging on the ground.

Hank squatted down and laid his books on the ground.

He didn't move a muscle, waiting for the bird to feel at ease. It took a cautious step forward. Hank held his breath. The bird took another step. And another. Each time it paused, turning its head sideways to look at him.

Slowly, Hank held out his hand, palm facing upward. He'd learned to do that on the streets when he met a stray dog. It was less likely to bite, maybe because it could tell you weren't going to hit it. Might be the same for birds, Hank thought.

The bird stopped and took a half step backward. It cocked its head first one way and then the other. Then it started forward again. Hank's legs were beginning to tingle. He puckered his lips and made kissing noises, trying to hurry the bird along. "Come on, fella," he said gently. "It's all right. I won't hurt you."

Suddenly the bird was right next to him. Hank could see its chest fluttering with the pounding of its heart. There was no blood on the injured wing, but, from the way it was bent, he was pretty sure it was broken. He reached out and touched the bird's back. The feathers were soft and warm.

I can't leave you here, Hank thought. He knew he couldn't take the bird back to the Olsons'. Mr. Olson would think it was stupid to keep an injured bird, and Mrs. Olson would want to fry it for supper.

Surely Mr. Givens would know what to do. He was a teacher. He knew everything. And when Hank brought the bird in, Mr. Givens would understand his tardiness. It would be all right.

Carefully he picked up the bird. It was heavier than it looked. He opened his coat and tucked it inside. It felt warm against his ribs.

Gingerly Hank gathered his books and walked as quickly as he could without jostling the bird. Soon he was in sight of the schoolhouse. The yard was empty, as he knew it would be. Even without a watch, he could tell it was well after eight o'clock. He walked up the steps and opened the door.

Mr. Givens was standing at the front of the room. He looked up as Hank walked in. "You're late," he said.

"I know, sir," Hank said. "I'm sorry, but . . ." He started to open his jacket to remove the bird.

"No buts!" Mr. Givens shouted, smacking his desk with his ruler. The noise startled the bird. It leaped out of Hank's hands onto the floor, where, flapping its good wing wildly, it made its way under the teacher's desk.

"What in the blazes?" Mr. Givens cried.

"It's a bird, sir," Hank said, trying to run after it, but finding it difficult to maneuver between the crowded benches, where the rest of the students sat laughing and shrieking.

Mr. Givens was furious.

"It's hurt, sir," Hank said. "I thought you would know what to do."

Mr. Givens bent down and snatched the bird from under

his desk. The bird pecked hard at his hand, breaking the skin and drawing blood. Mr. Givens swore under his breath. A hush fell over the room. His jaw tightened. He raised his hand, and Hank was afraid he might wring the bird's neck. Then, as though suddenly he had become aware of all the eyes watching him, he stopped. Grasping the bird firmly in two hands, he stalked to the back of the schoolroom, opened the door, and tossed it into the yard.

Hank was too stunned to move. He wanted to run out and pick up the bird, tell it he was sorry. But he couldn't. He just stood there, as though his feet had set root in the schoolhouse floor.

"Sit, Mr. Donohue," Mr. Givens said sternly.

Slowly, jerkily, Hank walked to the front of the room, where he sat with the first-level students. He could feel his classmates' eyes on him as he went.

"Class, let us resume our lessons," Mr. Givens said. His face was red with exasperation, and a small smear of blood from his hand stood out starkly against the white of his shirt.

5

Hank couldn't concentrate at all on his schoolwork. Mr. Givens called on him repeatedly, and he was unable to answer a single question. He could hear the older boys snickering from the back of the room, but he didn't care. He was waiting for the morning break, when he could go find the bird.

When finally they were released, Hank hurried out to the yard. He was too late. Matthew and his gang had gotten there first. They were poking at the bird with sticks, trying to get it out from under the steps, where it was hiding. When it did dart out one side, to get away from their prodding, Matthew grabbed it and tossed it to one of the other boys. They were using it as a football, throwing it back and forth. The bird was terrified, Hank could tell. It flapped its one good wing and squawked and pecked at the boys, but they only laughed.

"Stop it!" Hank yelled.

"Make me," answered Matthew, catching the bird and preparing to throw it again.

Hank couldn't stand it. In a rage, he flew at Matthew, head down, butting him in the chest and knocking him flat. He expected Matthew to get up and come at him. He almost wanted him to. But Matthew was too busy trying to get his wind back.

Hank didn't wait. He picked up the bird and took off across the yard. He didn't even go back for his books or his sketchbook.

Emily came after him. "You all right?" she asked. "Mr. Givens was angry. Can I touch the bird? Poor thing. What are you going to do with it? Are you going to keep it?"

She was such a chatterbox. Usually it didn't bother Hank, but now he just wanted to be alone. He shrugged and kept going.

"It's perfectly awful what those boys did." She was panting, trying to keep up.

Again Hank shrugged.

"What are you going to do now?" Emily asked. "Where are you going?"

"Don't know," Hank said.

"Can I come with you?" Emily asked.

Hank shook his head. He didn't want company. Besides,

he didn't want Emily getting into trouble with Mr. Givens on account of him, never mind with Mrs. Dewhurst. Emily had a hard enough time convincing the old bag to let her go to school, even though school and church had been part of the agreement with the home. If she got a note from the teacher, that might be the end of it. And Emily was smart. She could do something with an education. Not like him.

Hank stopped and looked at Emily. Her eyes glistened with held-back tears.

"I'll be all right," he said, and he turned and headed down the road, away from school.

The bird was still. For a while Hank thought it might be dead, but then he found he could feel its heart beating. He smoothed its feathers and held it gently against him. He could hear the boys in the school yard yelling after him, taunting him. "Sissy!" they hollered. "You'd go home to your mama, crybaby, but you ain't got one!" Laughter. No matter that he had just taken the biggest bully in the school in one blow. No matter that he had *not* cried. He wasn't like them, and that was sin enough.

He walked slowly. When he got to the spot where he'd found the bird, he stopped. He looked around to see whether any of its family might be about, wondering where it was, but there was nothing but dust and wind in the prairie grass. He sat down on a rock and put the bird in his lap. It settled in as though his lap were a nest, and began to look about. Its wing was hanging limp, and it had bent and broken feathers after the rough handling by the boys. It was a wonder it was still alive.

"Hard to say which of you looks worse." The voice startled him. He whipped around, one fist raised, holding the bird with the other. He was even more startled when he saw the figure that went with the voice. It was the woman from the pasture road.

"Didn't mean to scare you," she said. Her voice was gravelly and deep. Hank looked at his feet. He felt a little foolish.

"Broken wing," she said, looking at the bird. "What happened?"

"Don't know," Hank said. "It was broke when I found it."

"Broken," the woman said.

"What?"

"His wing was broken when you found him."

"Yeah," said Hank. "It was. But it wasn't all messed up like this until those boys at school started playing catch with it."

The woman's dark eyebrows rose sharply, and she pinched her lips together. "Ball?" she said.

"They were trying to keep it away from me."

"Why would they be doing that?" she asked.

"I don't know," he said. " 'Cause I'm an orphan, I guess."

The woman eyed him sideways, as though she were sizing him up. "He seems to like you," she said. "The grouse."

"It's a he?"

"Yes. You can tell by those yellow bars over his eyes."

"What'd you call him again?" Hank asked.

"A grouse," she said. "Sharp-tailed."

"Sharp-tailed grouse." It made him feel better, somehow, to know its proper name.

He turned back to the woman. "Who are you?" he asked.

"Molly," she said. Her voice sounded a bit like a rusty hinge. "McIntire," she added. Then, "Molly McIntire," as though she was not used to putting her name together out loud—or talking at all, really.

Hank regarded her more closely. She looked to be a mother's age. Her long brown hair was flecked with white. It was pulled back haphazardly and twisted into a knot of sorts. Strands hung down around her face and over her eyes, but she seemed not to notice. She had a long thin neck and brown eyes touched with gold that glistened in the daylight. Her face was brown and freckled from the sun, and her cheeks pink from the wind. She was slender, and she wore an old barn coat and a brown skirt that came to mid-calf and was tattered around the bottom. Her brown leather boots were sturdier than you might expect to see on a woman. Up close, Hank saw that her walking stick was carved and painted. Her basket, which she had placed on the ground, securely held a young fox.

"You?" she said. She was standing quietly, her head cocked to one side. It reminded him of the bird.

"What?" he said.

"Got a name?"

"Oh," he said. "Sure." Then he realized he still hadn't answered her question, and he added, "Hank. Donohue. Hank Donohue." Jeez. Now he was doing it.

Molly nodded. "Irish."

"Mmm," Hank said.

"Well, let me see your friend there, Hank." She reached out for the bird. Hank handed him over.

She ran her long bony fingers along his back and wings. The bird struggled a bit, but Hank got the feeling he wasn't afraid, just sore.

"Splint ought to do it," she said finally. "Come on with me, then." She handed the bird back to Hank and picked up the fox. She started away across the field.

Hank stood watching until she turned around and waved for him to follow. "Come on," she said again. "Get a move on."

Hank nodded and headed after her. He didn't know what to make of her. She was so peculiar. He wondered whether he should be afraid of her. He remembered the story his father used to tell about Hansel and Gretel and the witch with the gingerbread house. But he decided Molly wasn't a witch. And she seemed to know about birds. Besides, he had nowhere else to go.

6

Molly looked back from time to time, but she didn't say anything. Hank followed along, holding the bird, which kept looking about as though wondering, as he was, where they were going. Mrs. Olson's warning to stay away from Molly—"she's crazy"—nagged at him.

It seemed like forever before a small house came into sight. It was more of a cottage, really, Hank thought. It was painted white, with a wide front porch and trim carved in curlicues around the eaves. "Gingerbread," Molly called it. Hank gulped.

A large stone barn stood down a slope in front of the house. There was a fenced pasture, too. As they got nearer, Hank could make out the shapes of animals there. Where he had expected to see horses and cows, he saw—something else—animals with gray coats and large ears, and antlers you could hang your hat on.

"Mule deer," said Molly. "They come here hurt. Most get better and go on their way."

She walked up to the barn and unlatched the door. It squeaked open on its hinges. Inside was the most amazing racket Hank had ever heard. As his eyes adjusted to the dimness, he could see why. The barn walls were lined with makeshift cages, and each cage housed birds of different sizes and descriptions. Many bore signs of injury. Wired in place inside each cage were branches where the birds could perch. Some of the cages held only one bird, others held many. Some of the birds looked to Hank to be in pretty bad shape.

Hank felt his mouth drop open in surprise. The bird in his arms began to stir and look about, turning his head this way and that and fluttering his good wing. Hank wondered whether there were any other sharp-tailed grouse in the barn.

"Here," Molly said. She put down her basket and took the grouse from Hank. She carried him over to a table against the far wall.

A large black raven sat on the table and eyed the grouse curiously. "Shoo, Poe," Molly said, waving her hand in the black bird's direction. The raven cawed once and hopped down from the table, stalking off, apparently with hurt dignity.

"He gets jealous," Molly said.

Hank nodded. The bird toddled awkwardly, and Hank realized his tail feathers were missing.

"Now," she said, more to the grouse than to Hank, "let's see what's going on with you."

Her voice was softer when she was talking to birds, Hank noticed. He watched her work the bird's wing, testing the bones with her fingers. She checked the other wing, too, and felt all along his body.

"Just a simple dislocation, I think," she declared finally. "A couple of weeks, and you'll be off and flying," she told her patient. She attached a splint to the wing—"to keep it from bending," she told Hank—and secured it to a bandage she'd wrapped around the bird's body. That way the wing was stable, but he could still use it to keep his balance, she said. She left his other wing free so he could move it if he needed to.

When she finished, she placed the bird gently into a small crate and latched the door shut. "He will feel safer in there," she said.

Hank followed her around the barn while she checked up on some of her other patients. Poe stalked along behind her.

"Where'd you learn to do all this?" Hank asked.

Molly paused, then went on with her work. "I was a nurse," she said. "In the war. I learned just about everything there." She paused again. "Mostly I learned to prefer animals to people. Animals can be cruel, but they don't pretend otherwise." She opened a cage that housed a cat-sized black creature with a white stripe down its back. "A skunk is a skunk," she said. "You know who you're dealing with." There was a hardness in her voice, and Hank wondered what had put it there.

When she was done in the barn, Molly put the fox in a small pen outside. "I'll deal with you later," she said. She gave it water and food, then headed toward the house. "Right now it's teatime," she said. She held out her arm for Poe, and he hopped up onto her shoulder.

The inside of Molly's house was as surprising as the outside. A brown rabbit with one ear chewed off, a three-legged squirrel, a dog with one eye, another that appeared to be whole, and countless cats all made their home in her living room. A flowered sofa, ragged from the cats sharpening their claws in the fabric, sat beneath windows on one wall. A braided rug lay in the space between the sofa and the hearth of a large stone fireplace. Embers of a dying fire glowed through the ash. It was cool in the house, despite the air having warmed outside. Books of all shapes and sizes filled shelves built into the wall on each side of the fireplace. The house struck Hank at once as both chaotic and neat.

"Come into the kitchen," Molly said. "I'll put the kettle on." She dipped some water from a bucket and poured it into a cast-iron kettle. She stoked the fire in the stove and went to fixing a mixture of leaves, which she threw by handfuls into a chipped china teapot.

"Sit," she said, nudging a cat from a chair by the table. She sat down opposite him and folded her hands in front of her. "Won't they miss you?" she said. "At school?"

"Nah," said Hank. "Wouldn't anybody much care if I went or not." He shrugged. "I'm not much for learning anyways."

"I doubt that," Molly said. "You strike me as a clever young man."

Hank blushed and looked at his bare feet. His nails were rimmed with grime, and there was mud caked between his toes. He was glad Molly couldn't see them. "Only reason I go at all is because the home says I have to."

"The home?" Molly asked.

Hank told her about the train that brought the orphans from New York, and about the placing out.

She nodded. "I've heard of it," she said.

He told her about his brother, Peter, and how Mr. Olson's beatings drove him off. As he spoke, a cat jumped up and curled itself into his lap. Absently, he began to scratch behind its ear. It lifted its white chin toward the ceiling and purred loudly.

"She likes you," said Molly. She got up and poured the tea, adding a small dipper of honey to each cup. There was no milk. The tea was strong and earthy, but also hot and soothing, and it warmed him through.

He couldn't remember the last time he had talked so much. Molly sat and listened and nodded. He hoped she would tell him something of herself, of the war maybe, but she didn't.

He finished his tea and put down the cup. "Guess I'd better go," he said, though he didn't really want to. He stood up slowly and shoved his hands into his pockets.

"Where will you go, then?" Molly asked. "Back to school, or to the Olsons'?"

Hank wasn't sure.

"Seems to me neither one is expecting you right now. I have some work to be done around here, and I could use a strong boy." She put her hands to her head then, as though she had just remembered something important. "What am I thinking?" she said. "A growing boy like you needs more than tea to keep him going." She got up and went to the icebox.

His stomach began to rumble at the thought of food. He hadn't eaten since the night before. "Okay," he said. "I guess I can stay for a little while."

7

Molly took a roasted chicken out of the icebox. She cut off one leg for herself and sliced a stack of meat for Hank. She cut some thick pieces of brown bread and piled the meat between them. Next to the sandwich she placed a mound of sweet pickles.

Hank was surprised to see she would eat a bird, what with her barn full of them and Poe perched on the chairback watching her, but when he asked her about it, all she said was, "You ever meet a chicken you wouldn't eat?"

Hank had to admit that he hadn't.

"Well, then," Molly said. She picked up the chicken leg and bit off a dainty portion.

Hank couldn't remember the last time he had eaten something so delicious. Once, at the home, for Christmas some rich people had brought food for the orphans. It had been good, but there had been only enough for a mouthful or two for each of them.

After lunch, Molly took him out to the barn. She showed him how to feed and water all the birds, as well as the assorted animals in pens behind the barn, and the mule deer in the pasture.

She had chickens and a cow and horses, too, like Mr. Olson, and pigs. But Hank was most interested in the Model T Ford she had covered with a tarpaulin in the shed.

"Can I see?" Hank said. Molly nodded, and Hank carefully lifted the tarp. The auto was black and carefully polished despite being covered up.

"It's yours?" he said.

"Mmm," said Molly. Then she added, "It was my father's."

"He gave it to you?"

"He doesn't need it anymore," she said. "He's ill."

"How come you have it all covered up?" Hank asked. "If I had an automobile, I'd drive it everywhere."

"I'd rather walk," she said. There was something in her voice that told Hank not to ask any more questions.

"It's real handsome," he said, and pulled the tarpaulin back down.

When Hank was done feeding the animals, it was well past time for school to be out. He said goodbye and ran most of the way back to the Olsons'.

It was getting dark by the time he got there. He was out of

breath, and his ears were burning with the cold. The lamps were lit in the kitchen; he could see Mrs. Olson at the stove. There was a light in the barn, too. Mr. Olson must be brushing down the horses. He'd be hearing it for being late. He should have thought up an excuse, but none came to mind now. He'd never been good at fibbing. He decided to go to the barn first and get started on his chores.

"Where you been, boy?" Mr. Olson barked when he saw Hank.

Hank shrugged.

"You answer me when I speak to you," Mr. Olson said. His voice was low and threatening, and his lips were curled back against his gums, showing his teeth. Hank could sense the animals shifting nervously in their stalls.

He turned and looked at Mr. Olson. Might as well get it over with. "I went for a walk," he said.

"A walk!" Mr. Olson came close. He towered over Hank, so Hank had to tip his head back to see the old man's face.

"Yes, sir," he finally managed.

"From what I hear, your walk started about midmorning." He glared at Hank, daring him to deny it.

"Yes, sir," Hank said. "It was a long walk."

Mr. Olson raised his hand. Hank didn't flinch.

"Matthew Brown's father came by."

Hank didn't answer.

"Do you know who Mr. Brown is?"

"No, sir," said Hank.

"He runs the feed and grain store in town," Mr. Olson said. His voice came out in a hiss. "If Mr. Brown is unhappy with me, do you know what happens?" He didn't wait for Hank to answer. "He comes up short on my orders, that's what," he said. "He runs out of seed corn. He has a sudden increase in the price of feed." He inched closer to Hank and looked down on him. Then he lowered his hand, as though he'd decided Hank wasn't worth the effort. "Bad enough that useless brother of yours tangled with his boy. Now you start." He stared at Hank, pursing his lips as though he couldn't think of anything bad enough to call him. Finally he said, "I have told Mr. Brown that it won't happen again. I expect I won't have to go back on my word. Now you can finish your chores. Then it's off to your room. You can think about what I've said while Mrs. Olson and I have our supper."

Hank turned away so Mr. Olson wouldn't see him smile. He patted the chicken sandwich he had tucked inside his shirt. Eating Mrs. Olson's cooking today would be more of a punishment than not eating it.

8

Hank finished his chores slowly. He wasn't eager to go into the house. He would rather stay out in the barn with the animals—even the cow—than be inside, where Mr. and Mrs. Olson made him feel more alone than when he was by himself. He understood how Molly felt about her animals, why she preferred their company to people.

He sat down on the milking stool. Through the open barn doors, he could see the Olsons eating at the kitchen table. He leaned his head back against the cow's flank. She shifted her feet and switched her tail, then stood still.

On a ledge by her stall, Hank noticed a jackknife folded up and just lying there. He wondered how it was that he hadn't noticed it before. He went over and picked up the knife. The handle was made of horn. It was just like the knife his father used to use when he sat by the fire at night, whittling. Hank pried out the blade. It was a bit rusty, but there was a sharpening stone there, too.

He spit on the stone to wet it and went to work sharpening the blade. Surely if it was Mr. Olson's knife, he wouldn't mind it being sharpened. Probably doesn't even remember it's there, Hank told himself.

He found a fat stick on the floor of the barn and sat back down on the stool. He turned the stick this way and that, trying to see what his father might have seen.

Hank had marveled at the way his father could bring pieces of wood to life. It was as though there were people or animals hidden in the wood, and it was his father's gift to find them. He had always wanted a knife like his father's, had begged his father to let him hold the knife just once, but his father had always said no. "When you're older, son," he'd said, "then I'll show you how."

And now he was older, but his father wasn't around to show him. He threw the stick on the ground and spit in the dirt. He folded the blade back into the handle the way he'd seen his father and Peter do so many times, holding the sheath in his fingers, careful not to put his fingers in the way of the blade, and slipped the knife into his pocket.

Hank stood, and only then realized how stiff he was. He ached all over from his run-in with Matthew, and earlier with Mr. Olson and the cow. He sighed. He had better get inside, or the Olsons would be wondering what was keeping him.

The kitchen was warm. Hank thought about stopping by the stove to thaw his hands, but Mrs. Olson's icy stare told him he wasn't welcome. He walked past the table and to the back hall, where the narrow staircase led up to his room. He went to the washbasin and rinsed the grime from the barn off his hands.

He took out Molly's sandwich and ate it slowly. He savored each mouthful, and wondered whether he would ever be able to visit her again. It was odd, he thought, how having such a wonderful time with her had left him feeling so empty now.

He lay on the bed and pulled the covers up to his chin. He shivered. Not long ago Peter had crawled under the covers with him, adding his blanket to Hank's, and they had huddled together for warmth. But after Peter left, Mrs. Olson had removed his bed linens—for spite, Hank supposed. As though it were his fault.

That night he dreamed of home, of his mother peeling potatoes in the kitchen of their small tenement, and of the smell of cabbage boiling in the kettle. Peter was there, working his figures at the table by the stove, and his father, too, whittling.

In the dream, his mother promised to read to him. He had loved to listen to her read. Her Irish lilt had curled around the words, adding a richness to the stories.

The Olsons did not read. There was not a book in the house, except the family Bible, and that was not read but merely kept for recording births and deaths—including the deaths of the three Olson infants, three years apart, at birth. Hank had not read it, but after they heard the Olsons mention the babies during a fight, Peter had.

"If you'd let us move to California with my sister where it's warm and dry, my babies would still be living instead of lines in the family Bible," Mrs. Olson had said bitterly.

"You'd have me give up everything I've worked for, everything my father worked for, to head out to God knows where?" Mr. Olson had hollered back. "Heaven knows what we would have done. You think I didn't want my sons to live, woman? You think I didn't want sons to work the farm with? To take over when I'm gone?"

"There isn't going to be anything to take over when you're gone, old man," Mrs. Olson said, "between the drought and your drinking."

Mrs. Olson had started crying then, and Mr. Olson had stormed out the front door, slamming it behind him in disgust.

In his dream, Hank heard a door slam. He looked up from his mother's kitchen table to see Mr. Givens standing in the room, the grouse in his hands. Hank tried to get up, to run to Mr. Givens and take back the bird, but he couldn't move. He looked for his mother, but she was gone. His father was gone, too, and Peter. He was alone in the room with Mr. Givens and the bird. Only it wasn't Mr. Givens anymore, it was Mr. Olson. He was reaching up to take hold of the bird's head, as though he was going to wring its neck. But before he could, a hand grasped his arm. It was Molly. Carefully she lifted the bird from his hands. She ran her long bony fingers along the bird's back and wings. Then she held it up in front of her and blew into its face. The bird gave a cry and flew away. Then Mr. Olson was gone, and Molly was holding Hank's hand.

9

When Hank awoke, sunlight was pouring through the window. He lay in bed, watching the shadows on the ceiling. He felt almost warm. For a moment, he expected to hear his mother singing in the kitchen as she made breakfast.

Then he heard heavy footsteps on the stairs and realized where he was and what had happened. He was in his bed at the Olsons', and he had overslept. Mr. Olson was growling outside his door. Hank's heart began to pound. There was no escaping.

The door to his room flew open. Mr. Olson towered over him by the bed. He looked down. His mustache was yellow with tobacco smoke. His eyes were bloodshot. Hank could smell last night's moonshine on his breath. "You sick, boy?"

Hank shook his head.

Mr. Olson reached down and tore back the covers. "Well, then," he bellowed, "what are you doing in bed?"

Hank swung his legs over the side and stood up, trying to stay beyond arm's length of the old man's fury. It was no good. Mr. Olson grabbed him by the scruff of the neck and shoved him toward the door. There would be no attempt at cleanliness today.

He scurried down the stairs and grabbed his coat off the hook. Barefoot, he headed to the barn. At least there he would be alone. By the position of the sun in the sky, Hank figured it was too late to get to school. And anyway, after yesterday he guessed he wouldn't be welcome in the school yard today.

The cow was waiting for him. Her bag was full, and she was lowing mournfully. Her tail switched back and forth when she saw him coming. Was she glad to see him?

"You'll have to wait your turn," Hank said. "Chickens first, then pigs, then you. If you behave yourself." The cow mooed again.

"Oh, now we're best friends, are we? Ha!" He spit in the straw. "We'll see."

He walked out to the chicken coop, leaving the cow bellowing miserably behind him. The chickens, too, were waiting. He filled the pail with feed and went in, latching the door behind him. The rooster eyed him menacingly.

"Sorry I'm late," he said, spreading the corn and watching them scratch and peck for their breakfast. He gathered the eggs, then carried the pail of slop out to the pigs, who grunted with pleasure. When he was finished, he took a deep breath. "Okay, cow," he said, turning toward the barn, "your turn."

He grabbed the milking pail off its hook on the wall and set the stool down next to the cow. She was still complaining loudly. Her bag was not so much fuller than it would have been an hour earlier, he figured. It was only his tardiness she was annoyed at. He shook his head. "Dumb cow." Then he smiled and patted her flank.

"Don't like change much, do you?" he said. "You want things to stay the same forever." It was what his mother used to say about him. "Well, they don't," he said, sitting down heavily on the stool and placing the pail on the floor beneath her. "So you'd better get used to it."

He put his head against her side and reached down to begin milking. He grabbed her teats firmly and began to pull. To his surprise, the milk let down right away. The cow stood contentedly, looking back now and then as if to say, "It's about time you figured this out."

Hank milked until the pail was full, then got up and rubbed her nose. "Thanks," he said. He wished she had a name, so he could call her something besides "cow," but the Olsons weren't ones for naming their animals. Cow. Horse. Dog. Even he didn't have a name. He was only "boy."

"What do you think?" Hank said. "How about I call you Mabel?" One of the matrons at the home had been named

Mabel. Something about it seemed to fit the cow, he thought. The cow blinked. "All right, then. From now on, it's Mabel." He gave her nose a last rub, picked up the milk and eggs, and headed to the kitchen. He hadn't lost a drop of milk. The Olsons ought to be happy about that, anyway. Ought to, he thought, but wouldn't.

He sighed. He wondered whether some people just chose to be angry and bitter. His mother had lost babies, too, after all—both girls—and her heart had been broken each time, he knew. Yet still she managed to sing.

Mrs. Olson was up and grumbling when Hank came in with the milk and eggs. She was wiping soot from her hands onto her apron. "Had to start up the fire in the stove myself, thanks to you," she said.

"Sorry," said Hank, though he wasn't really. It wouldn't kill her to stoke the fire herself just once. "No dirt this morning," he said, lifting the pail up for her inspection.

Mrs. Olson raised an eyebrow and grunted. "So? You think you deserve a medal? Huh!"

Hank put the milk pail and eggs on the table and headed for his room. He would be too late for school, but perhaps he could go by Molly's. He wished he hadn't left his sketchbook at school yesterday. For the first time in a while, he felt like drawing.

He had gotten up too late to see Molly on the pasture road. He wondered, as he walked through the fields to her house, whether she would be home yet from her rounds. But when he got there, he found her out in the bird barn.

"Hey," he said.

Molly smiled. "Hey, yourself," she said. "Don't you have school?"

Hank shrugged. "I got up late. Then my chores. Mr. Givens hates tardiness. And after yesterday . . ." All excuses. The truth was, he would rather be at Molly's than at school.

Molly looked at him a minute, as though trying to decide what to do. If the Olsons found out he was there instead of at school, she might get into trouble, he thought. And he knew she held education in high regard. But finally she said, "Might as well make yourself useful, as long as you're here. There's a rake in the corner. You can clean out the grouse's crate for starters, then work on the rest of them."

The grouse looked better this morning. The gleam was back in his eye, and he was eating and preening his good wing. Hank carefully raked out the crate and spread clean straw on the floor. He gave the bird fresh water and feed, then closed the door and watched for a while as he scratched around and nestled into the straw.

He spent the rest of the morning cleaning up after the other birds, while Molly worked at changing dressings and tending broken bones and other injuries, clucking and singing to each bird as she went along. Hank couldn't remember the last time he felt so at ease.

When they were done in the barn, they went to the house and cleaned up. Molly had soup cooking on the stove, and she fed Hank a steaming bowlful. It was thick and rich and tasted grand. She cut off a piece of dark brown bread, which he used to soak up the last of the broth.

"More?" she asked when his bowl was empty. Hank, his mouth still full of bread, just nodded, and Molly ladled out another helping.

"You can't just stop going to school, you know," Molly said. She was sitting across from him, watching him eat. A cat was weaving in and out between his legs, purring loudly.

Hank looked at her. "Mr. Givens don't teach me nothing," he said. "Thinks I'm stupid."

"Are you?" she asked. "Stupid?"

"Not as stupid as Matthew Brown," he said. Molly raised an eyebrow. Hank shifted in his chair and looked at his feet. That wasn't the answer she was looking for. Besides, Matt wasn't stupid, just mean. "I don't know." He shrugged. "Don't have time for books since Peter left. Doesn't seem much point."

Molly opened her mouth as if to say something, but then she stopped and took a spoonful of her soup.

"The Olsons wouldn't be happy if they knew you were here," she said finally.

Hank nodded. "The old lady don't care for you much."

Molly smiled. "People don't like what they don't understand," she said. "They don't understand me."

"They think you're crazy," Hank said, and wished as soon as it was out that he hadn't said it.

Molly smiled again. "I hear I'm a witch," she said.

"Yeah," said Hank. "That's what they say." He swallowed another mouthful of soup. "You ain't, though." He paused and looked at her over his spoon. "Are you?"

She laughed outright at that, then covered her mouth with her hand, apparently surprised at the sound of it.

Hank laughed, too. It felt good.

Hank went to Molly's for the rest of the week. He worked in the barn, watched Molly tend the animals, helped her in the kitchen. He even baked bread. Poe still regarded him suspiciously, but Hank decided that was just his nature. The rest of the indoor animals seemed glad to have Hank there.

He went back to the Olsons' in the afternoon, about the time he would have gotten out of school. They never asked him how his day was, so he didn't have to lie.

But the following Monday, as he was heading out the door, Mrs. Olson stopped him. "If you're not going to school, you'll at least make yourself useful here."

Hank's heart sank.

"Thought we wouldn't find out?" Mrs. Olson said. "It's a small town. Word gets around. I don't know what you are doing with your days, but you haven't been in school."

Hank allowed himself to breathe again. At least they didn't know he had been going to Molly's.

"Sit down and eat," Mrs. Olson said. "You'll need a good breakfast if you're going to get any work done."

He sat and waited while Mrs. Olson melted a pat of lard to sizzling in the frying pan and broke in half a dozen eggs. A gray cloud began to rise from the pan as she tended the coffee that was boiling over on the stove. A ribbon curled up from the oven, where, Hank guessed, the biscuits had just passed from golden brown to their usual scorched black. "Good," he thought, was a matter of opinion.

After he choked down his breakfast, following it with the last of his burnt coffee, Hank went out to the barn to see what Mr. Olson wanted him to do. The old man was hitching the horses to the wagon. Mabel mooed and switched her tail when Hank came in. Hank winked at her, but didn't say anything. Mr. Olson wasn't one for being friendly with the animals.

Hank climbed up into the wagon. He could tell Mr. Olson was already in a foul mood. He scowled as he tightened the harnesses on the horses, which were shifting and acting generally nervous. Hank knew just how they felt.

Finally Mr. Olson swung up onto the seat of the wagon and flicked the reins. The wagon started with a jolt. Hank held tight to the sides. It was going to be a long day.

10

Hank thought he knew hard work. In the time he had been in Nebraska, he had hoed the field, dug potatoes and picked cabbages, pitched hay and slopped pigs. But none of that was worth a lick stacked up against shocking corn.

Mr. Olson drove the wagon to the edge of the cornfield. "Get out," he ordered. "We'll start here."

Hank climbed down and waited. He still wasn't sure what they were going to do.

Mr. Olson handed him a knife with a long flat blade. It was longer and wider than Hank's arm, and was straight at the tip, as though the end had snapped off, but he decided it had actually been made that way. It was heavy, and he noticed that the blade was nicked in a few places.

Running his thumb along the edge, he could tell it was dull, too.

Without a word to Hank, Mr. Olson began counting off rows of corn and marking them with the heel of his boot. Twelve rows in this direction, twelve rows in that.

"All right," he hollered to Hank from twelve rows down, "this'll be the first shock."

He pushed his way through the corn to the center of the square he'd made, and wrapped a green stalk around the inmost clump. Then he drew his knife and swiftly sliced through the stalks. The stalks stood in the dirt, leaning against one another, forming a tepee shape.

"You start there," he said, pointing to the first of the rows he'd marked off. "Three or four at a time. Then bring them over here and lean them up against this here bunch."

Hank looked at the corn. He looked at the enormous knife. He knew better than to ask questions. So he bent over and began sawing at the cornstalk with the knife.

"Not like that!" Mr. Olson shouted. "You got manure for brains?" He thrashed his way through the corn to where Hank was standing. "Like this!" He snatched the knife out of Hank's hand and pushed him aside with his shoulder. Then he raised the knife high, bent at the waist, and, grabbing the stalk and pulling up with his left hand, brought the knife down with his right, severing the stalk near the base in one swift motion. Then he straightened and handed the knife back to Hank. "I'll be working the other end of the field," he said. "Don't cut your hand off."

Hank knew the old man wasn't concerned for his safety. If Hank cut off his hand, he wouldn't be much use in the field.

He watched Mr. Olson drive away. Then he raised the knife, bent as Mr. Olson had done, and grabbed hold of the stalk. He brought the knife down with a thud against the cornstalk. Where the old man had cut the stalk cleanly with one blow, Hank had managed to bruise it and make a small cut. He raised the knife again. In three more blows, he had cut clear through. When he had cut three stalks, he gathered them together. They were taller than he was, and top-heavy. As he walked, they slipped and toppled in opposite directions, tripping him so that he stumbled several times. Finally he got them to where Mr. Olson had tied the center clump together, and leaned them up against it with the butt ends down.

Hank sat on his haunches and wiped his brow with his sleeve. He could hear Mr. Olson across the field, cutting and carrying, cutting and carrying. At the rate he was going, he'd have the rest of the field done before Hank finished his one small corner. Hank knew what that would mean: half rations for half work.

Today he actually felt grateful for the wind. It wasn't a warm day, but he was sweating already, and blisters were beginning to form on his hands. The leaves of cornstalks had scraped his arms and face, which stung as though he had rolled in a nest of red ants. The wind, in spite of the dust it threw in his eyes, was the only relief.

Mrs. Olson came out about midmorning with a water jug and cold biscuits and ham. For once Hank didn't care how salty and tough the ham was, or how hard the biscuits. He was plain hungry, and any food at all would do. It wasn't the kind of hungry he had known on the streets, the hopeless kind that gnaws at you all day, like a rat eating you from the inside out. This was the kind of hungry you get only from working hard with every inch of yourself. This was the kind of hungry you earned.

Hank had finished his first square and gone on to several more. Mr. Olson surveyed his work and grunted. For a moment Hank thought he might have pleased the old man, but after Mr. Olson had swallowed his biscuits and washed them down with a swig of water, he said, "Should have had twice as much done by now. Think we have all the time in the world to do this?"

Hank ached all over. His hands were scratched and blistered. He wanted to haul off and sock Mr. Olson right in the gut, but he didn't have the strength. Besides, it wouldn't have done him any good.

He sat on the edge of the wagon bed and squinted into the sun. Out along the pasture road, he saw Molly walking back toward her house. He wanted to wave, but he feared Mrs. Olson's reaction, so he just watched her pass down the road. He couldn't tell whether her basket was empty or full.

She kept her eyes on the road as she walked along. But just as she was moving out of sight behind a stand of cottonwood trees, she lifted her walking stick and, without breaking stride, tipped it ever so slightly in his direction. She had seen him.

Hank glanced around quickly to see whether Mr. or Mrs. Olson had noticed, but they were caught up in bickering over the corn crop and whether or not they were going to break even this year, or have to sell the farm and move to California. "As if anyone would buy it," said she. "You'll sell it over my dead body!" said he.

Hank smiled to himself. He pictured Molly heading back to her place, her basket holding some poor creature, then mending its bones, bedding it down, going back into her house with Poe for tea and bread in her warm cozy kitchen.

His thoughts were interrupted by Mr. Olson's heavy hand on his shoulder. "Dawdled long enough, boy," Mr. Olson barked. "Back to work!"

11

They worked until the sun went down. Hank thought in the middle of the afternoon that he would have to stop. His knees were wobbly, and his arms were aching. His blisters had long since turned to raw open sores on his hands. When he bent to cut the stalks, he could hardly straighten, his back was so sore. But he knew he couldn't stop, so he kept on going: bend, pull, cut, lift; bend, pull, cut, lift.

He let his mind wander. He thought about the grouse and wondered how he was doing. He thought about Peter. Where was he now? Had he gotten to New York? Perhaps he had already made his way to the children's home and told them about Mr. Olson, and they were coming back right now to get him. Finally, his thoughts settled on a song his father used to sing. The tune seemed to fit the rhythm of the task at hand, so he let it run in his mind over and over as he worked.

He could hear his father's rich tenor in his head. He imagined his father working there beside him, with his strong back and his hard callused hands, belting out the chorus.

When he finished a verse, he put down the knife and carried the bundle over to the rest. He leaned the new stalks against the others, placing them evenly to make a balanced shock. He found he could go for longer periods without looking around to see how much more he had to do. One shock at a time, one verse at a time. That was all.

When at last he did look up, he saw Mr. Olson not too far away. His shirt was unbuttoned and soaked with sweat. He took off his hat and wiped his brow with his sleeve as he gazed off into the distance. Hank wondered what the old man was looking at on the horizon. But Mr. Olson just put his hat back on and bent again, and Hank could see the blade of his knife come up over the tops of the corn before it dropped down swiftly to slice through another stalk. He can cut six to my one, Hank thought. Then he thought, I'd better get back to work, or there'll be a price to pay, and he bent and began again.

He was repeating the last verse of the song when he heard Mr. Olson bark, "Boy!"

He looked up without standing, so he wouldn't have far to duck if the old man raised his hand.

"You're daydreaming!" bellowed Mr. Olson.

"Yes, sir," Hank said.

"I said, you can knock off for the day. Mrs. Olson will have supper waiting."

"Yes, sir," Hank said. He was still trying to stay at arm's length. His fingers had been holding the knife so tight for so long he had trouble getting them to open to release it. He toted the last of the stalks over to the shock. Hank could feel Mr. Olson's eyes on him. He waited. He knew he would have something to say about his shoddy work, or how slow he was.

Instead the old man gave Hank a rough pat on the back. "You put in a good day's work, boy," he said.

A good day's work. Hank straightened. He gave the shock a final shake to make sure it was sturdy and eyed it to check the tilt of the sides so that if it ever did rain, the water would run down the sides and not rot the corn before it was put up for the winter. In the short time he had been in Nebraska, he had learned that corn was a farmer's most important crop. Without corn, you couldn't feed the animals, and without the animals, you would have no milk, no eggs, no meat, and you'd have to pull the plow yourself. He climbed up into the back of the wagon and looked out over the field as they pulled away. The field seemed larger than it had that morning. Maybe now he was measuring it by the amount of work, rather than by the square foot. He wondered how enormous it must be in a year when there was no drought.

12

Hank stayed in the barn, currying the horses, while Mr. Olson went to the pump to wash up. He could hear the handle squeak as Mr. Olson primed the pump, and then the water as it came splashing out and splattered on the porch floor. It sounded delicious. Though his arms ached to the bone, he brushed the horses down with as much speed as he could manage. He fed Mabel, scattered some grain for the chickens, and headed for the pump himself.

The water was icy. It made his fingers ache as he held his hands under, one at a time, and let it pour over his blistered palms. Then he stuck his head under and let the water gush down his neck and run in little rivers down his back. He took off his shirt and splashed water on his arms and chest and face. He didn't stop until Mrs. Olson rapped on the window and hollered, "Don't you know there's a drought on?"

He dried himself with his shirt. Then he shook his head like a dog that has been swimming in a pond, and the water flew from his hair, leaving dark spots where it sank into the dry, bare wood of the porch.

Dinner was on the table when he got inside. He hardly noticed the smell of burnt rolls and scorched fat from the fried pork chops. He was too hungry even to taste the food. He just shoveled it in, barely stopping to chew before he swallowed. His stomach seemed like a bottomless pit. But finally, after two or three helpings, it felt full, and he pushed his plate away and sat back.

Mr. Olson was chewing noisily, his arms resting on the edge of the table, his utensils raised, ready to attack his meat again once his mouth was empty. Mrs. Olson had one hand in her lap and was staring at her plate. No one spoke. No one ever spoke at the Olsons' table. It was so different from his mother's table, where there had always been discussion of the day's events and laughter and storytelling. And where the rolls were never blackened on the bottom.

He sighed. "I'm going to bed, then," he said, standing up and carrying his plate over to the sink. Nothing to scrape off for the pigs tonight.

Mr. Olson wiped his mouth with the back of his hand. "We'll be out in the morning first thing," he said through a mouthful of half-chewed roll. "You'll need to get your chores done early, so see you don't oversleep."

"Yes, sir," Hank said. He was almost out the door when he heard the old man add under his breath, "If I'd had some real help, we'd be half done by now. Seeing as how we don't have near the crop we should." He said it as though even the drought were Hank's fault.

Hank tightened his grip on the rail at the bottom of the stairs. Once, his father had taken him and Peter to an amusement park. They had ridden a roller coaster for the first time. They sat in the little car and held tight to the crossbar as they went up and down and round and round on the rickety wooden tracks, until Hank was sure he would be sick. Peter and their father had shrieked and laughed, but Hank had held on so tightly his knuckles had turned white. He hated the unexpectedness of it. He would just get used to going up when the coaster would crest the hill and plunge down, or side to side. After the ride was over, his knees felt weak, and his stomach was queasy for hours.

That was how he felt now. He had grown accustomed to Mr. Olson growling and smacking him. Then, today, out in the field, he had felt as though they were working together—they were comrades. The old man had praised him, or at least not criticized him, when they were done for the day. And then this!

Hank went slowly up the stairs. He didn't even take off his

wet shoes, just collapsed onto the bed and was asleep almost as soon as he closed his eyes.

It was a week before he talked to Molly again; a week before he got back to school. He and Mr. Olson worked together out in the field as if they were a team. The roller coaster was going up a long incline. It was a pretty smooth ride, but Hank knew eventually it would plunge down out of control again.

In the meantime, he found he enjoyed farmwork. He liked the way it made his muscles feel. And his muscles were growing, getting stronger, meatier. Sometimes, when he was getting dressed, he looked in the small mirror over his dresser and bent his arms at the elbows, balling his fists and flexing his muscles like a strong man at the circus. He wished his father could see him now. Hank remembered his father pressing his scrawny arm between his thumb and forefinger and saying, "My little man. Look at those muscles, Mama."

When finally the field work was done, Hank was almost sorry. He would much rather have been out working than in Mr. Givens's classroom, facing daily humiliation—and Matthew. They finished on Saturday. The next day, Sunday, they would rest.

They went to church, of course. Mrs. Olson put on her Sunday dress and hat, and she insisted that Mr. Olson wear his black suit with a black necktie and a starched white shirt that barely stretched across his shoulders and belly. The collar was so tight that his neck bulged around it and reminded Hank of an overstuffed sausage. Hank was forced to wear the clothing he'd worn on the train: knickers, brown dress shoes, a white shirt, and a jacket—all three sizes too small, at least—and woolen socks so scratchy they felt as though they were filled with straw. Mrs. Olson made him comb his hair and slicked down the cowlicks with grease, just as she did to Mr. Olson. Mr. Olson actually winked at him while she did this. As though being forced to endure this torture together gave them a bond.

He felt pretty foolish, and he was certain he looked it, too. He must have been the only boy his age who still wore knickers. Matthew Brown wouldn't be caught dead in them, he bet. But knickers had been doled out at the home for the boys riding the train, handed down from some of the city's finer families. Never mind that his had been snug when he got them, and that he had grown inches since then. Or that his shoulders were practically bursting through his shirt, they'd gotten so big from all the farmwork. That made him feel kind of proud, really. But it was uncomfortable. Halfway through Pastor Schiller's sermon, he could feel his fingers begin to tingle from lack of blood.

Emily was in church. So was Hattie. They smiled across the sanctuary at him, but they didn't make a move to talk to him. Hank sorely wished he could go off with them after the service, just to spend time with others who knew how it felt to be an orphan living among strangers. But even if he could overcome his shyness around Hattie, he knew the Olsons wouldn't abide it. And Emily was so busy watching over the Dewhurst brood he knew she wouldn't have time. It was on days like this that Hank missed Peter most.

13

After church, Pastor Schiller shook hands with everyone. Hank usually slipped by unnoticed, but today the pastor stopped him. "Heard from your brother, Hank?" he said. He spoke low, as though he didn't want the Olsons to hear him.

Hank shook his head. "No, sir," he said.

"He's a smart boy," the pastor said.

Hank wondered how the pastor knew. He nodded.

Pastor Schiller looked hard at him. "He'll be all right," he said. Then the pastor shook Hank's hand. He thumped him on the back and smoothed down his jacket.

"See you next week, Hank," Pastor Schiller said. Hank nodded and moved away. It was odd for the pastor to show him so much attention. Hank just wanted to get going.

He climbed into the back of the Olsons' wagon. It would

be a bumpy ride home. He'd found that if he relaxed and stayed loose, his bones took less of a jostling. He looked out over the side and watched the country pass by. What wasn't gray with dust was turning golden with early autumn. The sun was warm on his face, and it felt good even with the wind. He closed his eyes and turned up his face to soak in as much of the sunlight as he could.

On the way back to the farm, they passed through town. The streets were deserted, except for other churchgoers heading back home. There were little girls and boys dressed in their Sunday finery, walking with their parents, laughing and smiling. Some of the girls skipped along, and Hank imagined they were singing nursery songs as they went. Boys kicked pebbles and were scolded for scuffing their Sunday shoes. Hank's heart ached for his mother's scoldings. His eyes pricked suddenly with the memory. He swiped at them with the back of his hand.

When he reached into his pocket for the handkerchief Mrs. Olson had put there so he wouldn't embarrass her by sniffing—"The way boys do," she said—he stopped. There was something else in his pocket. He pulled it out. An envelope. It was addressed to him in care of Pastor Schiller. He recognized the handwriting. It was from Peter. He put it back in his pocket quickly, before the Olsons could see it. He couldn't wait to get back to the farm so he could go up to his room and read it. Was Peter coming for him? It had been wise to send the letter to the pastor rather than directly to the Olsons. They would likely have destroyed it rather than give it to him.

When they arrived back at the farm, he helped put the horses out to pasture, then ran up to his room. He took the letter out of his pocket. He hardly dared to open it. Would it contain plans for his escape? Finally he peeled back the flap and pulled out the letter. It was written in pencil on the back of a handbill advertising free food for hoboes who would come listen to a sermon.

"Dear Hank," he read. "Bet you are surprised to hear from me. I'm okay and I hope you are too. I am writing this from the boxcar of a train heading east. I traded my lunch for a stamp and an envelope, but it was okay because I got an old lady down the line to pity me, and she gave me a plate of fried chicken. Your big brother's still got it! I bet the Olsons are happy to have me gone and are treating you good. I don't have much time or much paper, but I didn't want you to be worried about me. I hope you are studying hard and not letting that bully Matthew Brown push you around. Take care of yourself, little brother. Love, Peter."

Hank put the letter down. His ears burned. The letter said nothing about Peter coming for him. And there was nowhere for Hank to contact him if he needed him—and he did need him. Part of him wanted to tear up the letter and throw it down the hole in the outhouse. But part of him wanted to hold it close forever. At least Peter was safe. Safe and thinking about his brother. He could wait knowing that, he thought. Peter was sure to come back. Wasn't he?

Carefully he folded the letter and tucked it under his mattress.

That afternoon Hank was restless. He ate Mrs. Olson's tough roast without tasting it. He did his chores in the barn without thinking about them. Irritated by the lack of attention, Mabel kicked over the bucket, something she hadn't done in a long time.

Hank went up to his room. He took out some paper he kept hidden in his dresser and punched holes in one side with a pencil. Then he pulled a lace from his Sunday shoes and threaded it through the holes to bind the pages. Not as neat as Peter's, but it would do, he figured.

He sat on the bed and tried to draw, but he couldn't keep his mind on it. He rolled up the sketchbook and stuck it in his pocket, then went downstairs.

"I think I'll take a walk," he said. Mrs. Olson looked up from her knitting and pursed her lips. Hank could see her trying to think of something he should be doing besides wasting time on a walk. Mr. Olson was snoring in his chair by the stove. An empty whiskey glass lay on its side on the floor next to him. Hank didn't wait for Mrs. Olson to answer. He turned and walked out the door.

His first thought was to go visit Molly. He could say he was there to see the bird. When he got there, though, no one was home except Poe, and apparently he wasn't in the mood for visitors. The bird cawed and flapped his wings in an irritated manner. So Hank took off, thinking maybe he would come upon Molly on her rounds. He walked through the fields and meadows, dry from drought and brown with dust. The land rose and fell like the swells in the ocean he remembered from back in New York.

After a time, he came upon a small shelter that looked as though it might have been a house once—when it still had a roof. He was thinking he might sit there and rest out of the wind, maybe sketch the old windmill that turned steadily with a squeak and a clatter near a small pond, which, surprisingly, still held water.

As he neared the place, he noticed a horse tethered nearby. Someone was sitting in the doorway. Was it Hattie? It was! On her lap was a large gray cat. She was scratching its chin absently with one hand and holding a book in the other. She seemed to be in another world. Hank stopped. She hadn't seen him yet. She would have had to turn around. He wanted to call to her, but she looked so peaceful there, he didn't want to disturb her. Besides, she had always made him feel shy—she was so smart he felt dumb around her. And he got all tongue-tied. So he sat down on a hump of dried grass, took out his sketchbook, and began to draw.

After a while, Hattie put down the book and looked off across the field. She put her hands to her lips one at a time and balled them into fists and blew on them. Hank had forgotten until then just how chilly the wind was.

Hattie looked different from the way she had at the home, but he supposed they all did. Her hair had grown out some, and curled in black wisps. Her face was tan from the sun, and her cheeks, which had always been pale, were pink from the wind. He wondered what she was reading. He wished he had read more books so he could walk up to her and say, "What are you reading? Oh, sure, I read that."

He was still watching, trying to get up the nerve to talk to her, when she picked up the cat and stood. Quickly he lay down behind the mound he had been perched on. If she saw him now, she might think he'd been spying. She mounted the horse, then turned and rode off. Hank couldn't decide what amazed him most: how pretty she'd become, or that she could ride a horse.

When he was sure she was out of sight, he sat up and leaned back against the mound. The dried grass pricked his back through his shirt. He looked at the picture he had drawn. He wished he'd had time to finish it.

He felt a little foolish now that he hadn't spoken to Hattie. Why hadn't he? His cheeks burned with more than just cold. He knew what Peter would say: "Hank loves Hattie. Hank loves Hattie," in a singsong way. He closed his sketchbook, rolled it up, and stuffed it back in his pocket. Then he headed off in the direction Hattie had taken.

When he got to the Jansens' house, the horse was in the

barn. Hank wondered what time it was. The Olsons would be missing him for sure, but he didn't care. He wanted to see where Hattie lived. He would only stay a moment. Then he would head back to do his chores and see whether Mrs. Olson had saved him any supper.

It was beginning to get dark, and there was a warm glow coming from the window. Inside, Hank could see Hattie and Mr. and Mrs. Jansen in the living room. Mr. Jansen was at his desk, and Mrs. Jansen was sitting in a chair by the fire, stitching patterns in cloth. Hattie was reading again, with the cat on her lap. Seeing them there, together, Hank felt a wave of sadness wash over him. They were just like a real family, like the family he'd had once.

He sank down on his haunches and leaned back against the house. He felt tears well in his eyes, then spill over hot against his cheeks. Baby! That was what the boys at school would say, what Peter would have said. But he couldn't help it. At that moment, he would have given anything to have Peter there to call him names and tell him to grow up. Sometimes he thought the loneliness was worse than the back of Mr. Olson's hand.

A sudden gust of wind turned his tears icy. Hank shivered. Slowly he stood up. Inside, a dog began to bark. He wondered if it had sensed his presence. Mr. Jansen called for it to quiet down. Then, when it didn't, Hank heard footsteps nearing the window where he stood. He saw Mr. Jansen walking to the window. For a second, he thought their eyes met.

Quickly Hank ducked below the sill and ran back the way he'd come. He didn't stop running until he reached the old shanty where he'd first seen Hattie. Then he bent over, hands on his knees, to catch his breath before continuing to the Olsons'.

He'd seen no sign of Molly while he was out. He swung by her place on the way back, but the windows were dark. Poe was still flapping about in the yard. There was a spooky feel to the place. Hank told himself he'd stop by tomorrow after school and make sure everything was all right.

14

It was full dark when Hank got back to the house. There was a lamp glowing in the living room window. Mrs. Olson would be there, tapping her foot in time to her knitting needles, impatiently waiting for him to return. She would be ready with complaints about the lack of firewood, the cow needing milking, the supper going cold. Mr. Olson would be lying drunk on the sofa in front of the fire.

Hank desperately didn't want to go inside. He wondered whether this was how Peter had felt the night he lit out. He wondered, too, whether his brother ever wished he hadn't left, ever felt, like him, that the loneliness was worse than the beatings.

He took a deep breath to brace himself against the pending storm of harsh words. He climbed the steps and opened the door to the kitchen. It was cold. The fire in the stove was out. He'd be blamed for that, too.

"Jo!" Mrs. Olson's voice cut through the air like a scythe as she tried to wake her husband. "Jo! The boy's back." Then, when he didn't answer, too drunk for even her sharp tone to reach, she muttered, "Oh, for pity's sake. I have to do everything myself around here. Boy! Come here, boy!"

Hank felt a bit like a lamb leading itself to slaughter. "Yes, ma'am," he said. He walked slowly into the living room. Sure enough, there was Mr. Olson laid out cold, and Mrs. Olson, knitting in hand, angrily peering up at him through the dim light.

"You're late, boy," she said. "Where've you been?" She squinted her eyes.

Hank shrugged. "Sorry, ma'am." Then, though he knew he shouldn't ask but was too hungry not to, he said, "Any supper left, ma'am?"

"Supper?" she cried. "Supper? He wants to know if there's supper! Did you hear that, Jo?" Mr. Olson snored loudly. "Your supper has gone to the pigs!" she shouted. "If you can't be here when supper is served, you'll go without. You think I have nothing better to do than cook for people who aren't here to eat?"

"Yes, ma'am," Hank said, though he couldn't see that she actually did have anything better to do. "I'll be milking the cow and going to bed, then."

"Oh no you won't. Not until you've filled the coal bucket, split some firewood, and tended to the rest of the animals. Mr. Olson's ill. He's in no condition to do anything," she said.

Ill? Was that what she called it?

"And the chicken coop needs cleaning—all the manure shoveled up and dumped out behind the shed. You'll find the shovel and wheelbarrow in the barn."

Hank's heart sank. He didn't know much about chickens, but he figured it had been half a year since the coop had been cleaned. It would be midnight before he got to bed, and now that Mr. Olson didn't need him in the field, there'd be school in the morning. After two weeks off, Hank had mixed feelings about going back. He wasn't looking forward to seeing Mr. Givens or Matthew Brown.

Hank took his jacket and cap off the hook by the kitchen door, lit the lantern, and headed out to the barn. At least Mabel seemed happy to see him, though he could tell she was put out that he had arrived so late in the day to do his duty. Still, she was agreeable and kept all her hooves on the ground.

The pigs had already been fed, he noticed. Mrs. Olson, it seemed, had been so eager to give them Hank's supper that she had actually gone all the way out to the barn to feed them herself!

Cleaning the chicken coop was a miserable job. Hank took off his shirt and tied it over his mouth and nose to keep out the chicken dust and the strong smell of ammonia, which made him cough and stung his nose. He found two small eggs in a corner of the coop and slipped them into his pocket.

By the time Hank finished, the house was dark. He hung the shovel on its hook on the wall and headed toward the house. He trudged up the narrow staircase to his room. There was some cold water left in the washbasin on his dresser. He washed his hands, then sat down on the bed and took the eggs out of his pocket. He was so hungry his hands shook as he broke the eggs open one by one, lifted them to his lips, and let the contents slide across his tongue and down his throat.

It wasn't much of a supper, but it was better than nothing. His stomach rumbled thankfully. He put the shells back in his pocket to dispose of in the morning. Then he blew out the lantern and lay down. He didn't bother to take off his clothes, which were fairly covered with chicken dust and probably smelled worse than the chicken coop itself.

15

When the sun came up next morning, Hank wanted to pull the blanket over his head and sleep for another six hours. He ached all over, and his throat still burned from the ammonia and chicken dust he'd inhaled cleaning out the coop. But he knew the Olsons would be awake soon and expecting their milk and eggs. He pulled on his shoes and headed downstairs.

Mrs. Olson was already in the kitchen, peeling potatoes. She looked up when he came in and scowled. "Don't you smell like the devil himself this morning," she said, wrinkling her nose and holding her apron in front of her face. "Out with you!" she said, pointing to the door. "You'd think you were raised in a barn." She waved the apron as though she were trying to banish the scent after him.

What did she expect, he wondered, after she'd made him

spend the night shoveling chicken manure? That he'd smell like clover?

He all but sleepwalked through his chores, waking up only after Mabel stepped on his foot. He was pretty sure she'd done it on purpose. He fed and watered the horses and scattered fresh grain for the chickens. The eggs were scarce this morning. Mrs. Olson would scowl some more. Nothing I can do about it, Hank thought. Not like I can lay them myself. He wouldn't tell her about the two he'd eaten raw the night before.

He picked up the eggs and the pail of milk and lugged them back to the house.

"Leave your clothes on the front porch," Mrs. Olson ordered, holding her nose. "Phew!"

"Here?" Hank said. "But someone might see me."

"No one's going to see you," she said. "Besides, you've got nothing we haven't all seen before."

Hank could feel his cheeks turning red. He didn't care for the idea of stripping in front of Mrs. Olson, especially right there on the front porch where anyone might come by. But he knew there was no point in arguing. He unbuckled his overalls and let them drop to the porch floor. He pulled them off over his shoes and started inside.

"Shirt, too!" Mrs. Olson said. "And the underthings. And those shoes! You smell like you've been rolling with the pigs!" Hank's cheeks burned redder. His ears were hot. He didn't move.

"Go on!" she said. "Get!"

Quickly Hank kicked off his shoes and peeled off his shirt and drawers. Holding his shoes in front of him, he ran through the kitchen and up to his room. He was about to put on his clean pants when Mrs. Olson hollered up the stairs to him, "Don't you go putting on those clean clothes until you've washed yourself, boy! Come back here and put some soap to you."

Hank groaned. He was cold and tired. He would be late for school at this rate, and he'd have an earful from Mr. Givens, who would already be primed, since Hank hadn't been there for so long.

He balled up his clothes and carried them downstairs, to where Mrs. Olson had set out a tub of lukewarm water by the pump on the porch. "Wash!" she said. "The rest of us have to eat around you. We don't need you drawing flies!"

Hank stepped into the tub. He rubbed himself all over with the harsh brown soap. He ducked his head and applied the soap to his hair, scrubbing hard with his fingertips, then rinsing as best he could. He jumped out and threw on his clothes, not even stopping to dry himself first.

He was shivering when he went in for breakfast, and he could see in the mirror by the door that his lips were blue with cold. Mrs. Olson had fried eggs and bacon and charred some toast by the fire. He broke off the edges, where the toast was pure black, and ate out the middles. The eggs were rubbery, and the bacon was underdone and fatty. A shame that some pig had given up its life for this, Hank thought.

The weather had warmed by the time Hank got to school. It was early yet, and boys and girls were gathering in the yard, shooting marbles, jumping rope, and playing tag. Off to one side, tethered to a hitching post in the yard, was the horse he had seen Hattie riding the day before. Hank felt as though his heart were jumping rope. Had Hattie finally come to school? He was standing there, wondering, when he heard Emily's voice.

"Hank, guess who's here? Hattie. She just came riding in on a horse. Can you believe it? Do you suppose it's her very own? It will be so good to have a girl my own age, someone who knows what it's like . . ."

Her voice trailed off, and Hank knew she was thinking about what it was like to be an orphan, to be living in a house full of strangers who couldn't care less, to be alone. Hank didn't want to think about it right then. He was glad Mrs. Olson had made him take a bath.

"Did you see her?" he asked. "What class is she going to be in?" As soon as he asked that, he was sorry. She wouldn't be in his class, that was certain. Hattie was one of the best readers and ciphers from the home. Even Mr. Givens had to see how good she was.

Finally the bell rang. Hank shuffled in behind the rest of

the boys. With Hattie being there, Mr. Givens didn't even seem to notice that he was back, and that was just fine with him.

Hank saw that Hattie was already seated. Third class. He wondered why she wasn't higher. He looked down at his feet so he wouldn't stare at her. Glancing up, he noticed Matthew sitting down beside her. He said something Hank couldn't hear, but from the look on Hattie's face, Hank knew it wasn't nice. His blood began to boil.

When everyone was seated, Mr. Givens introduced Hattie. "One of our orphan children," he said.

As though we're pets, Hank thought.

They recited the Pledge of Allegiance and the Lord's Prayer and read the daily Bible lesson. Hank could barely remember any of the words. He kept wanting to turn around and look to make sure Hattie was still there. He couldn't wait until the morning break, when they would be able to go out to the yard. This time he would talk to her, he decided. No matter what. Though he supposed every boy in the school would be wanting to talk to her.

Mr. Givens gave out assignments then, and most of the room went quiet as everyone got busy. The first and second classes were working with Mr. Givens on their recitations when a loud yelp interrupted them.

"What's going on here?" Mr. Givens shouted. His face went red, the way it always did when the class got out of his control.

"She stepped on my toe!" It was Matthew. It sounded as though he was crying—or trying hard not to.

"Is that true, Hattie?"

Hank turned around to see what was happening. Hattie nodded.

"Why did you step on Matthew's toe?" Mr. Givens asked.

Hattie shrugged. Probably because he deserved it, Hank thought.

"Come up here, Hattie, and stand in the corner. I will have to send a note home." He shook his head sadly as Hattie made her way to the front of the room. "This is no way to begin your scholarship at Disappointment Creek," he said.

Hank's cheeks burned with embarrassment for Hattie. Even though he was sure Matthew had asked for it, he knew how it felt to stand in the corner. And she was sure to catch it in the yard now. Matthew wasn't one to forget about a thing like this. Hank looked back. He could see Matthew grinning, as though he had won some great victory by getting another orphan in trouble.

16

When the break finally came, Hank watched while everyone filed out. Hattie kept her eyes straight ahead as she walked from her place in the corner to the classroom door. Hank stood last and went to the door.

Outside, boys and girls were lined up to use the outhouses. Hattie had gone over to check on her horse, and Emily had followed. Hank took the steps in one bound and stood at the bottom, watching. He could hear Emily's chatter from where he stood.

"Oh, she's beautiful. Is she all yours? I think Sheba's an absolutely lovely name. You ride her all by yourself?"

Hattie smiled patiently. "She's not all mine," she said. "She's really Elizabeth's." Hank supposed Elizabeth was Mrs. Jansen, since there were no other children where Hattie had been placed out. "But Elizabeth doesn't ride her anymore. Henry"—Mr. Jansen?—"says I should take her because she needs the exercise."

Hank was happy listening, and he could have stood there all day except that just then Matthew came out of the privy. Hank felt himself tense all over, like a coyote on alert for danger.

"Poor little orphans never seen a horse?" Matthew shouted.

"Leave 'em alone, Matt," one of his gang said. But Matthew wouldn't stop; Hank knew he wouldn't.

Hank walked slowly toward them, his hands in his pockets, his fists clenched tight.

"Ignore him," he said, stepping up close to Emily and Hattie.

Matthew kept pushing. "Nobody rides horses to school anymore, you know. Everybody rides bicycles. You will all have to go steal yourselves some. Wouldn't help, though. You ain't got no pa to teach you how to ride." He laughed.

Hank was spitting mad. He remembered what Mr. Olson said about getting into fights with Matthew Brown, but he hardly cared anymore. It was one thing for Matthew to insult him, but seeing him hurt Hattie was more than he could stand.

"Come on, Hank," Emily said. She was always one for avoiding trouble. "Let's go back inside."

"Yeah, Hank," Matthew said, "just go back inside with the girls. You ain't got no pa to teach you how to fight, either."

Suddenly Hank couldn't hold back. There was something about Matthew's meanness that filled him with rage. He was so angry he was shaking. He was blinded with it. All he could see was Matthew's freckled face, and he lunged for it. A crowd gathered around, but Hank was hardly aware of them.

Then he felt a hand on the back of his neck, and he was lifted up and away from Matthew, who was lying on his back, blood pouring from his nose and mouth. Mr. Givens held Hank tight by the collar, and reached down and pulled Matthew to his feet. The two boys glared at each other as they wiped their bloody noses on their sleeves.

But Hank wasn't done. "Why don't you go home to that pa you're always bragging on," he said. "Maybe he can teach you some manners."

Matthew directed a mouthful of bloody spit in Hank's direction. It landed with a splat on Mr. Givens's shoe.

Mr. Givens frowned. "You'll both be going home," he said. "And you'll be taking a note from me with you."

Hank swallowed hard. I don't care, he told himself. Matthew deserved it, talking to Hattie and Emily that way. But he did care. He could hear his mother's voice telling him that fists never solved anything. Besides, Matthew could throw a punch, but it was nothing to the back of Mr. Olson's hand. And what if the old man decided to get rid of him? What would happen to him then? He might never see Peter again—how would his brother find him?—or Molly, or Hattie. And what if he ended up someplace even worse than the Olsons'?

Inside, Hank gathered up his things and the note from Mr. Givens. He dared to glance at Hattie and saw her watching him. He thought perhaps he saw her smile. Or was she laughing at him? Pitying him? He had thought he was defending her, but now he wondered if maybe she was ashamed of him.

Hank couldn't bring himself to go back to the farm, so he walked to Molly's instead. He had wanted to check up on the place anyway.

When he got there, Molly was in the field with the mule deer. She was rubbing down the hind leg of one with some sort of poultice.

"Hello!" Hank called. He waved to her from the fence.

She turned and looked at him and smiled vaguely.

"I was worried," he said. "You weren't here yesterday." Still she said nothing.

"I've come to see the bird," he said. "The grouse."

She turned to him again. Finally she said, "He's gone."

"Gone?" Hank was surprised. "You mean he died?"

Molly shook her head. "I mean he's gone. Flew the coop. Went home. Gone."

"Oh," said Hank. He was disappointed, although he was glad the bird was better.

"What are you doing here?" Molly said. She sounded irritated, and Hank wondered if she wanted him to leave.

"I came to see the bird," he said. Hadn't he already told her that?

"I mean now," said Molly, as though she couldn't believe he didn't understand what she'd meant.

Hank had forgotten that he should have been in school. "I got in a fight," he said. "Mr. Givens sent me home, but I didn't want to go to the Olsons'."

"Why is it that nearly every time I see you, you've been in a fight at school?" Molly said sharply. "Don't you know that fighting never solved anything?"

Hearing his mother's words coming from Molly made Hank want to spit. Of course he knew it. But it didn't help to have Molly point it out while his nose was still smarting and his lip oozing blood. And didn't anyone understand that sometimes there was nothing else to do? You could let a bully get away with just so much. Surely even his mother knew that. He wanted to explain to Molly, to make her see.

"Do you think you're the only one with troubles?" she shouted, before he could respond. "You want to end up like him? Like Mr. Olson?"

Hank was taken aback by her outburst. Where had it come from?

She wasn't done. "You can't beat your wife and children

and then, when you lie dying, expect everyone to forgive you. No one will care," she said. Her voice sounded choked. "No one!" She stood up and ran across the field to the house. Hank looked after her. He felt sick to his stomach.

"Sorry I bothered you," he said, though he knew she couldn't hear him. "I won't do it again."

He turned sharply and headed off across the field, walking slowly at first, and then running, running as though he could outrun her parting words.

17

Hank was surprised when he found himself down by the railroad tracks. He hadn't given any thought to where he was going. He had run until he couldn't run anymore, then he had walked. He was hungry and his bare feet were sore and blistered. Molly's words had followed him. The anger in her eyes reminded him of Peter, and he was beginning to see it in his own reflection lately. Part of him wished he hadn't run, but part of him thought Molly should have understood.

He sat on a rock and looked around. There was a camp of sorts by a stream, where the hoboes slept, he supposed. But it was daytime, and the camp was deserted. He wondered if this was the sort of place Peter called home now. He pictured his brother hopping onto moving freight trains, heading toward freedom—away from the Olsons, from school, from him.

That was when it hit him, the realization that Peter wasn't

coming back. Why should he? What was there for him here? A man who beat him, a brother who meant nothing but responsibility. Hank didn't blame him for hightailing it. He might, too, if he weren't such a chicken. It was no wonder no one had much use for him. The Olsons, Peter, Mr. Givens, Hattie, and now Molly. His own parents had left him, after all. And even though in his mind he knew they hadn't chosen to get sick, in some part of his heart he felt as though they had abandoned him.

A train sounded. Hank could feel the ground vibrate under him. It would be passing by soon, he figured. He looked at the sky. The sun was edging toward the horizon. Mr. Olson would be looking for him to do his after-school chores. He stood, and only then realized how stiff he was from his run-in with Matthew.

He didn't want to go back to the Olsons', but he could think of nowhere else to go. There was no point in pretending that nothing had happened; the cuts and bruises on his face said it all. It would do no good to tell the old man that Matthew Brown had started it, or that he had been defending Hattie. He felt trapped.

Hank listened as the train came closer. Suddenly he couldn't take it anymore. He stood up and ran as fast as his feet would carry him to the tracks. He could see the train coming. It was louder than thunder, and it was going faster than he had expected. I'll get a running start, he thought. Then I'll jump and grab on.

As the train rolled by him, he looked for places on the side that he might hold on to, but every time he thought he saw one, it had passed before he could move. In the end, the train was gone, and Hank hadn't taken a step. He climbed up the bank and onto the track and watched as the train disappeared into the distance, leaving only a trail of smoke that the wind blew away.

When Hank got back, the old man was in the barn, mending a harness. He looked up and studied Hank's face, then returned to his work.

"Where'd you get them bruises, boy?" he asked, without looking up again. Hank couldn't shrug his response if Mr. Olson wasn't watching, so he had to say something.

"Fight, I guess."

"You guess? I think if I was in a fight, I'd know it."

"I guess," Hank said again.

"Don't suppose that fight had anything to do with Matthew Brown, did it?"

"Yes, sir," Hank began, "but—"

The old man didn't wait for him to finish. He stood up and lashed out with the piece of harness. The leather strap hit the side of Hank's face like a whip. It burned like fire. Hank clenched his fists, but he was too tired and sore to fight. And what good would it do? He'd had his chance. He could have hopped that train and ridden away forever, just like Peter. But he didn't. He couldn't even do that. Tears sprang to Hank's eyes, and he put his hands up to ward off another blow.

Mr. Olson towered over him, holding the harness ready to strike again. "I warned you," he said.

"I'm sorry," said Hank. He was crying full out now. Not just about the welt rising on his cheek, but about how impossible it seemed to do anything right, how no one understood, and how just plain lonely his life was. "I'm sorry," he said again. "I'm sorry."

A look of disgust crossed the old man's face. He spit in the straw. "Get!" he said. "Go up to your room. I don't want to see your face again today."

Hank looked at Mabel. It seemed to him hers was the only kind face he'd seen all day. She nodded in his direction and blinked twice. He wanted to go to her and throw his arms around her. He wanted to feel her warmth against his face. But he knew Mr. Olson wouldn't stand for that, so he turned and went into the house. He heard Mabel moo, then bellow loudly after what he figured was a smack with the harness from Mr. Olson. He longed to run back to the barn and let Mr. Olson have it, but he knew that wouldn't do Mabel, or him, any good.

It was days before Hank went back to school. He did his chores in the morning. Mrs. Olson put him to work chopping wood—enough to last three winters, Hank figured. By nightfall he was so tired he hardly had time to think about how miserable he was. In the morning he got up and did it all again.

The end of October came and went. Hank had dreamed of taking Hattie to the Halloween dance, but he'd hardly spoken to her since she started school, except to tell her, when he finally went back after the fight and she asked him, that he was fine.

He'd almost stopped thinking about Peter. His brother, like everyone else he'd ever cared about, was gone. That was all. The letter under his mattress had become a dream to him.

As fall moved on, he went through his days like a sleepwalker. Matthew hardly bothered to torment him anymore, because Hank didn't notice. Mr. Givens didn't call on him in school, because Hank didn't answer. Only Mabel could get his attention—by stepping on his toes, or by kicking over the milk pail.

Then one Sunday he heard Mrs. Dewhurst talking to another woman after church. "Her father's ill," Mrs. Dewhurst said. "She asked Matthew Brown to take care of the animals while she's away. She has a whole barnful. Imagine the vermin! If you ask me, it wouldn't be any great loss if Molly McIntire never came back."

She asked Matthew Brown to watch the animals? Hank felt sick at that. Did she hate him so much? What had he done? Then his sickness turned to anger. He didn't deserve it. He didn't deserve Molly's mistrust. He'd had good reasons for fighting. Why couldn't she understand?

He climbed into the back of the Olsons' wagon and wrapped his arms tightly across his chest. He could feel the jackknife in his pocket, hard against his leg. He would show them. He would show them all. This time he really would leave. He didn't need them. He didn't need anyone.

He would go to the Olsons' and scrounge some food, maybe some money. He'd say goodbye to Mabel. She was the only one who would miss him. And then he'd leave. He'd jump a train, or maybe he'd just hitch a ride in town. He didn't care where he went. It didn't matter.

It was cold, and the wind was especially fierce on the ride back to the farm. As though it were blowing in a change, his mother would have said. His ears burned, and his thin coat was doing a poor job of keeping out the chill. He blew on his fingers to warm them. He would have to wait for his chance to sneak off. He would take his sketchbook. Some dried meat—they owed him that much. He could wear his extra clothes so he wouldn't freeze.

In the meantime, he'd have to act as if nothing had changed. He put on his work clothes and went out to the barn. Mabel was glad to see him. He was grateful for the warmth of her breath—and her flanks.

"Hey, girl," he said. "I'm going to miss you."

She looked at him with her big brown eyes, and Hank felt that she understood.

"I wish you could come with me," he said. "But they'd be after me with the law for sure then." He rubbed her nose, and she licked his hand.

He sat on the milking stool and leaned against the cow. He couldn't bear the thought of going back inside. He pulled his cap down over his eyes and folded his arms across his chest for extra warmth. He was surprised at how calm he felt now that he had made his decision. A short nap, he thought, would help him stay awake tonight so he could slip out after the Olsons went to bed.

18

Hank woke with a start. Mr. Olson was standing over him, glowering.

"Boy!" he shouted. "What are you doing sleeping when there's work to do?"

It took Hank a moment to orient himself. His neck was stiff from leaning against Mabel, who was shifting nervously now that the old man was in the barn.

Mr. Olson kicked Hank's foot. "I'm talking to you, boy."

Hank blinked and rubbed his neck. Mr. Olson kicked him again.

Hank jumped up then. His heart was racing. The calm he remembered feeling just before he fell asleep was gone. He reached into his pocket and felt for the knife. His fist tightened around it.

Mr. Olson's eyes narrowed. He raised his hand as though he were going to strike.

Hank could feel the rage come over him. It was the same rage he'd felt when Matthew Brown had hurt the bird, the same rage he'd felt when Matthew had insulted Hattie her first day in school. He couldn't see anything except Mr. Olson's raised hand. He wanted to kill him.

Don't you know that fighting never solved anything? Molly's words rang in his ears. Do you want to end up like him?

Hank looked at Mr. Olson as though he'd never truly seen him before. He wasn't a big man, really, not all that much bigger than Hank. His eyes were bloodshot and sunken. His skin hung on his face, and it had a yellow cast to it. He hadn't shaved in days. He looked like one of the bums Hank and Peter had run across on the streets in New York. How could he have so much power? How had Hank let him?

Hank let go of the knife and took his hand out of his pocket. "Don't," he said quietly. "Don't ever touch me again." He turned then and walked toward the house. He wished Molly were here so he could talk to her, tell her he understood what she had meant. Tell her goodbye.

He went into the kitchen. Mrs. Olson was standing at the stove. He walked past her without a word and went up to his room. He would rest, then get up early and slip away as Peter had. It wouldn't do to let them know he was leaving. He didn't fool himself. He had won today's battle with the old man, but it wouldn't last. And Mr. Olson would never let Hank walk out. He needed him too much.

Hank slept later than he meant to and woke to a surprising quiet. Outside his window, the world had turned white. He'd never seen so much snow. Whereas before the wind had carried dust, now it whipped the snow so that the snow appeared to fall sideways, and Hank couldn't tell where the sky ended and the ground began.

His plan would have to wait. He couldn't head out for his new life in a blizzard.

He broke the skin of ice that had formed in the basin on his dresser and splashed some of the cold water on his face. He rubbed his wet fingers through his hair.

Downstairs, Mr. and Mrs. Olson were up and dressed. Mrs. Olson was mixing batter for pancakes. Mr. Olson was at the table, drinking coffee. Hank slipped on his coat and hat and, turning up the collar against the wind, stepped out into the storm.

The snow was blowing and drifting. It was piled high against the sides of the house, and Hank couldn't find the steps to the porch. He could barely see the barn. He plunged through the drifts, sinking up to his knees. The snow whipped against his cheeks, each flake a tiny needle.

Inside the barn, Mabel was snorting clouds of white steam. Hank stamped his feet to shake off as much snow as he could. His shoes were full of the stuff, but taking them off to empty them was out of the question in this cold. He rubbed his hands together, trying to warm them enough to do the milking. He put them against Mabel's flanks to draw some heat from her.

By the time he was done with his chores, it was snowing so hard he could barely make out the house across the yard. He ducked his head, pointed his feet in the general direction of the house, and hoped for the best. He'd heard of people freezing to death in snowdrifts only yards from their houses because it was snowing so hard they got lost.

Snow was glued to his lashes, and his coat and hat were plastered white by the time he made it to the porch. Mrs. Olson hollered at him for dripping on the floor, and for not putting a cover on the milk, so that it got full of snow on the way from the barn.

He shook out his coat and hat and kicked off his shoes by the stove. Then he stood and warmed his numb hands and backside until Mr. Olson told him to sit down because he was blocking all the heat. Soon, he told himself. Soon he would be gone. He wondered if they would be sorry.

Breakfast was warm, at least. Hank ate hungrily. There would be no school today. He would have to find some way to pass the time.

He went up to his room and took out his sketchbook. He flipped through the drawings. He settled on the one of Hattie. He imagined she was indoors, sitting by the fire, reading one of those books of hers. He sighed and pulled his blanket around him. There was frost on the windowpanes. The heat from the stove never made it up to his little room. He almost wished he could be out chopping wood. At least the hard work would warm him.

He scraped a patch of frost off the window and looked out. The snow was still coming down hard. He remembered seeing a pair of snowshoes in the barn. With those on, he thought, you could walk without sinking to your knees in the drifts. It was finding where you were going that you'd have to worry about. Maybe when the snow eased, he'd give it a try.

19

The snow let up after lunch. Mr. Olson was asleep, and Mrs. Olson was in the root cellar when Hank slipped out the back door to the barn. He'd bundled his few belongings and stuffed his pockets with biscuits and a bit of dried beef that he found in the kitchen. He took the snowshoes off the wall and fastened them on over his Sunday shoes, which he'd squeezed into because his everyday ones were still wet from the morning.

He said goodbye to Mabel. The cow reached out with her tongue and licked his hand. He rubbed her nose, and she mooed. He wondered whether she really knew he was leaving.

He wrapped Mr. Olson's scratchy wool scarf around his face and headed off toward the pasture road. It was cold, but finally the air was clean and crisp. Hank was glad to be out of the house, in the fresh cold air. He wasn't sure where he was going, but wherever he went, the wind would blow away his tracks and keep the old man off his trail.

Walking with snowshoes took some getting used to. He had to keep his legs wide apart so the shoes didn't bump against each other with every step. He hadn't gone too far before his legs began to get tired. His face was numb, and his fingers ached with the cold.

The usual landmarks were buried in snow, and Hank had trouble getting his bearings. The snow was falling again, and the wind was picking up. When he looked back, the farm was lost behind a curtain of white. Then he started to wonder whether back really was the direction of the farm, or whether he'd gotten turned around somehow and back was really forward. Since his tracks were blown away by the wind, he could no longer tell where he'd come from.

A familiar panic was beginning to rise in him—that feeling of being lost and alone. It reminded him of the day his mother died, and he and Peter first hit the street. "We have to go now," Peter had said. "We can't wait. They'll take us away. Who knows where we'll end up. But we won't be together, that's for sure. Ma wouldn't have wanted that." And so they had packed up what food and clothes they could fit into pillowcases, and left the tenement that had always been their home.

There were things Hank later wished he had remembered to take. His father's jackknife. The stuffed rabbit that he'd slept with for years when he was little, and that his mother had made clothes for. It was stored in a small trunk under the stairs. He wondered what had become of it. He wished he'd taken the photograph of his mother and father on their wedding day. They had looked so happy, his mother beautiful in her grand white dress, and his father with his curly black hair slicked into place and his mustache waxed.

It had been winter when his mother died, and snowing, but the streets of the city were never clean and white. Hank shook away the memory and looked around him again. It wouldn't do to stand there worrying: he had to move one way or another. He ducked his head into the wind and started off.

Hank felt as though he'd been walking forever. His toes throbbed with the cold. "That's good," he could hear his brother saying. "If they hurt, that means they ain't frost-bit."

He was no longer watching where he was going. It didn't matter, since he couldn't see more than two feet in front of him anyway. When his snowshoe snagged on a barbed wire fence, he was caught off guard and fell backward into the snow. It was a minute before he could get himself untangled and upright again. Then he took hold of the top wire and carefully felt his way along, figuring it might lead him to a barn or house.

After a while, his hand hit a wall. He felt his way along that to a door, found the latch, and opened it. He knew instantly whose barn he'd come to. Birds fluttered and called and squawked upon his entering, and a large black raven with no tail feathers strutted over and began to caw. Poe.

As his eyes adjusted to the dim light in the barn, Hank noticed that the place was a mess. The feed bowls were empty and the water frozen. The cages looked as though they hadn't been cleaned out in a while. Here and there a songbird lay dead. Where was Matthew Brown? Wasn't he supposed to be taking care of things? Served Molly right, depending on a bully to watch her place, Hank thought. But he put that out of his mind quickly and set about filling the food trays. The animals weren't to blame.

The water in the jug by the door was frozen. Hank lit a small fire in the woodstove and set a pail of snow on it to melt. There were fewer birds than he'd remembered, mostly those with permanent injuries. Hank wondered whether the mule deer were still in the pasture. If they were, they'd have to fend for themselves until the snow stopped.

When all the birds were fed, Hank allowed himself to sit by the stove and warm up. His clothes were soaked. He stripped down to his woolens and set everything to dry near the fire. The biscuits in his pocket were soggy crumbs. He emptied them onto the floor, where Poe devoured them. There was an old wooden chair near Molly's worktable. He pulled it up to the stove and sat down to rest. He gnawed on the dried beef and leaned back in the chair.

From the hard work and the heat of the stove, Hank was

asleep before he knew it. He opened his eyes when he felt Poe jump up, first to his leg, then to his chest. A sharp peck on his earlobe woke him fully. "Hey!" he cried. "That hurts! Get off!"

Poe, indignant, fluttered to the ground.

"Thank you," said Hank. He stood up and went to the window. It was dark outside, and the stove had gone out in the barn. He shivered. The Olsons would be wondering where he was. He could see the moon through the clouds. It had stopped snowing for the moment.

He felt his clothes by the stove. "Dry enough," he said to Poe. He turned his back to the bird, who was making him feel self-conscious, and put on his pants and shirt. He sat down and pulled on his socks and shoes. Poe hopped closer and pecked at the shoelaces while Hank tried to tie them.

"Shoo," Hank said, but the bird wouldn't budge. "Scram," he shouted, but Poe just tugged on one of the laces. He must think it's a worm, Hank thought. Dumb bird. The idea made him laugh.

Poe looked at him, then hopped away.

"Oh, don't get your feathers all ruffled," Hank said.

Hank put on the showshoes and headed out into the cold. The snow had drifted up against the door to Molly's house. He had to clear it away with his hands in order to open it. Inside, it was cold as ice. The animals had begun barking and mewing loudly as soon as they heard him at the door. Now they were frantically milling about him, trying to tell him, he was sure, how hungry they were and what a difficult time they had had. From the smell, he knew it had been a while since they had been out to do their business. He looked around in the darkness for a lamp and matches. He started a fire in the fireplace and lit the stove in the kitchen.

On the table was a note for Matthew. "Matt," it said, "the animals must be fed twice a day and the barn swept. Please let the dogs out when you come, and make sure they are inside when you leave. I will be home Sunday night."

So Matt had expected her to be home by now. And with the snow, he surely couldn't have gotten here from town today. He would have known better than to head out into a blizzard, Hank thought, unlike me. So where was she? Had she had an accident? Maybe she was caught in the storm.

He fed the animals and cleaned up their piles on the floor. Though he hated to go back out, he knew the cow must be miserable.

He headed back to the stable and found the horse snorting in an irritated manner. The cow just looked at him and bellowed a loud "Mooo."

"Okay, girl," he said, "I'm here." He pulled up the stool and set to work. He wondered whether Mr. Olson had noticed yet that he wasn't there to milk Mabel.

20

Hank went back to the house and put another log on the fire. It was past suppertime now, he figured. His stomach was telling him so. He supposed he'd better bed down on Molly's couch for the night. There was no way he could go anywhere in the dark, with the snow coming down the way it was again. Besides, the animals needed him.

He looked around in the kitchen for something to eat. The food in the icebox was turning green. He found some apples in the cellar and some dried venison, and there was plenty of fresh milk. The eggs he'd collected he would save for breakfast.

When he was full, he cleaned up and went into the living room to sit by the fire. But it was too early to sleep, and his afternoon nap had given him energy, so he was restless. Besides, he was worried about Molly. He noticed a letter lying open on her desk. He hesitated, but then went to the desk and picked it up.

"The funeral will be on Friday," he read. "I know you had no use for him, but Mother and I would like you to be here."

He flipped back to the first page. "Dear Molly," it said, "I thought you would want to know Father died last night in his sleep. Your visits these last few weeks meant a lot to him, I know. He spoke of them often.

"He spoke, too, of his many regrets—the drinking, the way he used to hit Mother and us children. I think he was truly sorry.

"As to the situation you asked about, yes, I think there is someone here in the city who can help you. Perhaps you can stop and see her while you are here."

Hank put down the letter. He'd read enough. No wonder she had been angry at him for fighting. Now she had gone off to her father's funeral and gotten caught in the storm. He could only hope she was somewhere safe and warm and not stuck in a snowdrift between here and her mother's. He wished he had taken the time to talk to her when he saw her last, instead of running off the way he did. She had said he wasn't the only person who had troubles. But he hadn't realized that she was speaking of herself. He hadn't been able to think about anyone else or anything but his own problems. Funny, he'd believed grownups never had problems. Wasn't that what being grownup meant? No, he thought now. Obviously not. He could have kicked himself for being such a fool.

Hank wondered what "situation" her sister was referring to. Maybe that was what had held her up longer than expected.

One of the cats rubbed against his leg. He picked it up and buried his face in its fur. It purred loudly. "Poor fella," he said. "You miss her, don't you? Well, don't worry. I won't leave you." The cat yawned and stretched and settled into his arms. He sat down on the sofa and let the other cats cozy in around him. Before he knew it, he was asleep.

It was cold when he woke up, and he was hungry. He stoked the fire and cut himself some cheese and bread. There were sweet pickles in a jar on the shelf, and he took out one of those, too. Then he sat on the sofa with the cats and ate.

Hank let his eyes wander over the titles of the books by the fireplace. He hadn't really looked at them before. It seemed as though Molly read about every kind of book there was: history, stories, science. He got up and went closer for a better look. There was a book with pictures of birds and descriptions of them. There was another with drawings of animals, showing all their parts, inside and out. And there were storybooks of all sorts.

One book in particular caught Hank's eye. It had the word "Poe" pressed in gold on the leather spine. He took it down and opened it. He ran his finger down the list of contents at the front: "The Pit and the Pendulum," "The Telltale Heart," "The Raven."

"The Raven"? He looked at Poe, who had hopped up onto the table and was watching him. Poe cocked his head and looked at Hank as though he wanted to hear more.

Hank sat on the sofa and began to read aloud:

> "*Once upon a midnight dreary, while I pondered, weak*
> *and weary,*
> *Over many a quaint and curious volume of forgotten*
> *lore—*
> *While I nodded, nearly napping, suddenly there came a*
> *tapping,*
> *As of some one gently rapping, rapping at my chamber*
> *door.*
> *' 'Tis some visitor,' I muttered, 'tapping at my chamber*
> *door—*
>
> > *Only this and nothing more.'* "

Hank wasn't sure of all the words, and he couldn't understand the Lenore character the narrator was talking about, but he was interested in the raven, who kept saying, "Nevermore." It was a spooky poem, though, and Hank found himself wishing someone else were there—someone besides Poe, whom he expected to open his mouth and say, "Nevermore."

The wind was blowing hard outside Molly's window, and now and then he could hear something—leaves?—hit the window and make a *tap-tap* sound.

He put the book down. When his father was alive, he had sometimes told him and Peter ghost stories, and Hank had liked listening to them when he was warm and safe in the living room, with his parents near. But he wasn't sure he cared to have this Poe fellow scaring him to death when there was no one around to save him from his own imagination.

He picked up the book again, and flipped through it looking for something that might take that *tap-tap-tapping* out of his mind. There was another one about Lenore, but it wasn't very interesting, something about a girl who died young. And there was a story called "The Pit and the Pendulum." That looked even scarier than "The Raven," so Hank decided to put Poe aside for now. He went back to Molly's shelf and tilted his head sideways to read the titles.

Hank's family hadn't owned many books. There was a collection of folktales his father had read to them, and his mother had a small book of poems she had brought with her from Ireland. Outside of the library, Hank couldn't recall ever seeing so many books in one place before. It hadn't occurred to him that people could collect books as though they were treasure.

His eye lit on another book that caught his fancy. *Oliver Twist*, by Charles Dickens. It was the story of an English orphan boy. He remembered suddenly that his father had been reading it to them just before he took ill. When his father could no longer read because it set him to coughing so bad, his mother made them return the book to the library. She wouldn't read it to them herself, she said, because it was too sad.

He took the book down and opened it. He didn't know where his father had stopped, so he sat down on the couch and began at the beginning.

21

Hank read well into the night and much of the next day. In the brief breaks in the storm, he made his way out to feed the animals and milk the cow and gather what few eggs the chickens saw fit to lay in that weather. The rest of the time he stayed indoors, trying to keep warm by Molly's fireplace. He was glad he'd paid attention the week he'd spent so much time with Molly, and learned how to boil an egg.

He longed for something else to eat and thought wistfully of his mother's corned beef and cabbage. But as he slowly worked his way through *Oliver Twist*, looking up words he didn't know in Molly's big, leather-bound dictionary, and reading some parts over and over until they straightened out and made sense to him, he decided that he was better off than poor Oliver, who couldn't get seconds of the gruel they fed the orphans and was put out into the street for asking.

His father's voice, which he thought he'd forgotten, came back to him as he read. He didn't want to stop reading for fear he would lose it again.

On the morning of the fourth day, Hank awoke to sunshine. The snow was blinding bright when he went out to feed the animals. The wind whipped across the field with a stinging force, and he still needed the snowshoes to make his way to the barn.

He was halfway there when he saw something dark in the snow ahead of him. He had to squint against the sun and blowing snow, but he was fairly sure that, whatever it was, it was alive.

When he got close enough, he could see that it was a large bird—a wild turkey, if he wasn't mistaken. And it was injured. There was blood in the snow. It reminded him of the grouse, the way it sat there with that trusting look in its eye. Hank wondered what it was about him that made these animals put their faith in him. He sure wouldn't if he were in their place.

The bird allowed him to pick it up and carry it to the barn. He put it on Molly's worktable and tried to examine it the way he thought Molly might. Once he got a good look at it, he could see the bird's wing was full of buckshot. Hank figured it would live, but he thought he ought to dig out as much of the shot as he could, and then bandage the wing to keep it still, as Molly had done with the grouse's.

He took a sharp penknife from Molly's table, and wiped the blade with alcohol to kill the germs. Then he set to work.

It took a good hour to get the wounds cleaned out. He wrapped the wing with the strips of white cloth Molly kept on the table for bandages, and set the turkey inside a pen. Suddenly Hank realized it was Thanksgiving, and that he was trying to *save* a turkey. He laughed out loud. He wished Molly were there so they could laugh together.

The other birds began making a fuss, wondering where their breakfast was, so Hank fed them and put out fresh water. He went to the stable and fed the horse and cow and scattered some grain for the chickens. By the time he got back to the house, he was pretty hungry himself, and the indoor pets were making noise, too.

It was two more days before the storm finally passed for good. Poe had taken to riding around on Hank's shoulder whenever he went out to the barn, and the turkey seemed to be getting better. It was eating and flapping about. Hank wondered how he would know when the bird was well enough to be let go.

That morning, while Hank was reading by the fire, he heard scraping and the noise of an engine. He looked out the window. Someone in a truck with a plow attached to the undercarriage was clearing the snow off Molly's drive. He couldn't make out who was driving. The truck stopped near the barn, and a man got out. He wore a heavy coat with a collar turned up over his ears and a hat tugged down so that his face hardly showed. Hank pulled on his own coat and put on his snowshoes and headed out to talk to whoever it was and see whether he had any news of Molly. He stopped when he got outside. A boy had gotten out of the truck, too. Even from the porch, Hank could tell it was Matthew Brown. The man must be his father. He ducked back behind the corner of the house. The last person he wanted to see was Matthew Brown. Besides, wouldn't they wonder what he was doing there?

"Stupid!" the man was saying. "She may be crazy, but she's one of my best customers. And you just leave her animals to starve? Idiot!"

Hank peeked around the corner. Matthew's shoulders were slumped, and he was looking at his shoes. For the first time, Hank felt sorry for Matthew Brown. He knew what it was like to be bullied. Now he saw that Matthew did, too. No wonder he picked on Hank and Hattie. He had to be more powerful than somebody. Who better than an orphan?

"What's the matter with you, anyway? Huh? Get in that barn and see if there's anything left alive."

Hank stepped out then. "Hey!" he called.

They turned, surprised.

"Hey!" Hank called again.

The man waved.

Hank ran over as best he could in his snowshoes.

"Who are you?" the man asked, pushing his hat back on his head. He had red hair, Hank could see now, and freckles, just like his son.

"Hank Donohue," he said. "I work for Miss McIntire."

The man raised one eyebrow.

"Actually, I'm minding the place while Miss McIntire is away," Hank said. He wanted to keep talking so Mr. Brown wouldn't have time to question him. "Except for last week," he added, because of course Mr. Brown would know that Matthew had tended the animals then. "I was tied up," he said. "Thanks, by the way." He looked at Matthew. "I know Miss McIntire was grateful. We would have been lost without you. But things are fine now. I was just on my way to check on the birds." He stopped and took a breath. He wondered how Emily managed to keep up her yammering without turning blue.

Mr. Brown looked at Matthew, then back at Hank. "Miss McIntire telephoned me this morning and asked me to come by and plow so she could get into the place," he said.

"She telephoned?" Hank said. He was relieved to know she was all right, but still he wondered where she was. He wondered, too, whether she'd asked about the animals and how Matt was doing taking care of them.

"Seems she got waylaid. Then the storm came. Couldn't get home. Was worried about the animals. My boy had been feeding them. Thought she was home by now." He eyed Hank suspiciously. "Guess she forgot you was staying here."

"Yeah," Hank said. "I guess. Matt and I talked about it," he added. "Remember, Matt? Last week at school. I guess maybe it slipped your mind."

Matthew looked stunned, and for a moment Hank thought maybe he wasn't going to back him up. "Oh," he said at last. "Yeah. Last week. Right."

Mr. Brown took off his hat and whacked Matt's head with it, sending the boy's cap into the snow. "Why didn't you tell me?" he said. He shook his head. "Fool boy." He put his own hat back on and straightened it on his head.

"Well, she expects to be getting in today, so I guess I'll take off," he said. "Get in the truck, boy," he said to Matt. He was still shaking his head as they drove off.

Hank watched them drive away. "Thanks," he called after them, and gave a wave that he hoped seemed casual.

All at once he was sorry that Molly was coming back. It meant he would have to leave. Running away hadn't seemed so scary a week ago, when he was angry. But now the idea of heading out to who knows where was terrifying. He looked across the white fields that seemed to stretch on forever and imagined himself walking across them in his stolen snow-shoes. He shivered, suddenly cold and already feeling lonely. He would at least wait until Molly got home.

22

It was well after noon when Hank heard a commotion in the yard. There were dogs barking and men shouting. He ran out to see what was happening.

Mr. Olson was there with his old hound dog. Half the town seemed to be with him. When Mr. Olson saw Hank, he started on a string of cursing, enough to make a hobo blush. He was obviously drunk. Hank stiffened. He was not going back. He couldn't go back.

Mr. Olson came up onto the porch and took Hank by the collar. "I ought to wring your neck, boy," he said. He hissed the words through clenched teeth. His face was white with rage. Hank could smell the corn liquor on his breath. He figured the old man hadn't lost much sleep over his being missing.

He realized then what it was that had made the old man

so angry when Peter ran off. It wasn't that he cared about Peter but that he had lost his power over him. That was what it came down to—power. That was what he wanted now. He wanted the whole town to see that Hank was his, that he controlled him.

Mr. Olson turned to the crowd and put up his hand. "This is him," he said. "Thank you all for your help. I'll take it from here." He smiled, but Hank knew there wasn't any good feeling behind it. He was angry and humiliated that a boy could run off and embarrass him that way. Mr. Olson would have been happier if they had found him dead in the snow somewhere, Hank figured. Then folks would have felt sorry for him, instead of laughing at him.

The people didn't seem eager to leave. They milled about in Molly's yard with their dogs as though they didn't quite know what to do with themselves. Hank noticed that Mr. Brown was there in his truck. He must have tipped Mr. Olson off. Even Mr. Givens was there. It surprised Hank that the teacher would go out in this weather to search for him. Maybe he figured it would look bad, the teacher not caring enough to help find one of his pupils, Hank thought. Maybe he was hoping Hank would turn up frozen in a snowbank.

Pastor Schiller broke off from the crowd and came up to the porch.

"Maybe the boy should see the doctor, Jo," he said. "Just to be safe."

"He don't need no doctor," Mr. Olson said. "I know what

he needs, and he'll get it when I get him home." Mr. Olson's grip on Hank's collar tightened.

"Now, come on, Jo," Pastor Schiller said. "It's been a long few days, what with you not knowing where the boy was. Worry will make you do things you might not do otherwise. The boy didn't mean any harm, did you, boy? Probably just got caught in the storm."

Hank didn't answer.

"Caught in the storm!" Mr. Olson laughed. "If he hadn't stolen my snowshoes, and lit out when there was still chores to be done, he wouldn't have been out in the storm. Only an idiot would head out into a Nebraska blizzard!"

"He's a boy, Jo," Pastor Schiller said. "Didn't you ever do anything stupid when you were a boy? Besides, he's never seen a Nebraska blizzard before."

Mr. Olson got angry then. "All of you go on home now," he yelled. "You too, Pastor. I'll handle this. He's my boy."

Hank bristled at the reference. His "boy." As though I were his horse, he thought.

The pastor looked at Hank, then at Mr. Olson. The crowd looked at Pastor Schiller as though waiting for him to act. Hank watched, too. Mr. Olson would be hard pressed to lay into him with the pastor right there and half the town standing by. But he'd been around long enough to know folks figured it wasn't up to them to tell anyone else how to raise their children—even if they weren't really their children, and were just poor orphans from the East. Some of them might even have figured it was a strong hand like Mr. Olson's that was going to wipe out those evil city ways.

He should run, Hank thought. Get while the getting was good. But his feet felt glued to the floorboards. And there was Mr. Olson's choking grip on his collar.

"Don't do anything you'll be sorry for, Jo," Pastor Schiller said softly. He looked at Hank again, then turned back to the crowd. "Come on," he said. "Let's go home."

Hank watched the pastor begin to walk away, and he felt an anger rise up in him. He had wanted, had expected the pastor to make things better, but he was turning his back and walking away. It was up to him, he realized. He had to do something.

"No!" he said. He was surprised at the force in his voice.

Pastor Schiller turned back. "What'd you say, Hank?"

Hank reached up and broke Mr. Olson's grip on his shirt. "I said no. I won't go back with him. You can't make me."

He stood still and straight and looked at the pastor. It was as though the whole crowd had stopped breathing. Even the wind had stopped to listen.

"He's mean," Hank said. "And he's crazy. They both are. And I won't live with them anymore. I don't care where I go. I won't go back."

"Why, you—" Mr. Olson began. He was looking at the driveway, and the whole crowd turned to follow his gaze.

Molly's black Model T was there. The crowd parted to let it through, then watched this new development.

Molly got out of the car and stood taking in the scene. A woman Hank didn't recognize got out from the passenger side.

"Hank," Molly said, ignoring Mr. Olson and Pastor Schiller and everybody, "you all right?"

Hank nodded.

Mr. Olson glared. "We was just leaving," he said. He took hold of Hank's arm and tugged him in the direction of the porch steps.

"I don't think so," said the woman who had arrived with Molly.

Hank twisted away from Mr. Olson's grip.

Molly smiled. "Let me introduce Mrs. Capwell," she said. "She's a representative from the children's home. She's come to check up on the boy." Molly paused and focused on Mr. Olson.

He looked pale, but he tipped his hat in the woman's direction. "Ma'am," he said.

Mrs. Capwell nodded. "Hello, Hank," she said.

"Hello," Hank said. He felt confused and embarrassed to be the center of so much fuss.

"I stopped by Mrs. Capwell's office while I was in the city," Molly said, looking directly at Mr. Olson. "Seems I wasn't the first to complain to the authorities about your treatment of the boy. Mrs. Capwell was already planning a visit. I thought I could help out by giving her a ride."

Someone had told them about me? Hank thought. He felt

almost giddy at the idea. He wondered who it could have been. Then he noticed Pastor Schiller looking awkwardly down at the ground, and figured he knew.

Now Molly and Mr. Olson were watching each other closely. Mr. Olson looked grim. Molly was smiling.

"We stopped by your place first," Molly continued. "Imagine my surprise when Mrs. Olson told us you were here." She turned to Mrs. Capwell and added, "I so rarely have visitors."

"Boy run off," Mr. Olson said. "I had word he was holed up here. Came to get him, is all. Sorry to bother you."

Molly smiled again. "Oh, no bother," she said.

"I'd be interested to hear from Hank why exactly he 'run off,' " Mrs. Capwell said. "Or from his brother, perhaps?" She looked sharply at Mr. Olson then, and Hank had a pretty good idea she knew Peter wasn't there. "Our records show there were two boys placed out with you, Mr. Olson." The way she said it, it was more a question than a statement, as though she was asking him to explain Peter's whereabouts.

Mr. Olson cleared his throat and looked around at the crowd in the yard. Did he think one of those people he'd just told to get out might help him? Most folks stared at their shoes, apparently embarrassed for him.

"These boys were bad seeds from the start," Mr. Olson said. He spit a glob of chewing tobacco into the snow. "Never should have sent them out here in the first place. Nothing but trouble."

Hank felt his face turning red. He wasn't surprised that Mr. Olson would try to blame him and Peter. But it just wasn't fair.

"That's a lie," he said. He could barely hear himself speak at first. He looked up and saw everyone leaning forward a bit, as if they were trying to catch what he said. He spoke again. "That's a lie," he said more loudly.

Molly's eyes flashed to Mr. Olson, and a look of satisfaction crossed her face.

Mrs. Capwell held up her skirts and climbed through the snow to the porch. "I know it is, Hank," she said. "We all know it is." She put her arm around his shoulder. "Now, if you'll come with me, we'll get this all straightened out."

Hank looked at Mr. Olson, who was glowering at him. He looked at Mrs. Capwell. What would become of him if he left with her, he wondered. Would he go back to the home? Would they place him out with someone else, someone who might be even worse than the Olsons? Mrs. Capwell seemed well-meaning and all, but how could he know the home would do better by him this time? And what about Molly? She had risked the well-being of her animals to stay in the city to see Mrs. Capwell. About him! He was that important to her, and he hadn't even known it.

"If you don't mind, ma'am," he said finally, "I'd just as soon stay here."

Mrs. Capwell and Molly looked surprised. Mr. Olson

smiled. "Now, that's a smart boy," he said. "Knows where his bread is buttered."

"No, sir," Hank said. "I mean here. With Miss McIntire." He looked at Molly. She had put her hand to her throat, as if she were trying to catch her breath.

"I don't think," she began. "But," she tried again.

"The thing is," Hank said, "I think you can use some help around here. I have a way with animals. You'll see. I've been taking care of things while you were gone. I even doctored a turkey full of buckshot. And Poe and I have become friends. And I'm reading *Oliver Twist*."

Molly laughed out loud at that. "*Oliver Twist*?" she said.

"Yes, ma'am. Edgar Allan Poe was too scary to read all alone."

Molly laughed again. "I know what you mean," she said. "I haven't read Poe myself in years."

She looked at Mrs. Capwell. "We can't make the boy leave in the middle of *Oliver Twist*," she said. "Can we, now?"

23

After the crowd left, Molly and Hank took Mrs. Capwell to town. She would stay in the hotel overnight before returning to her office to make her report.

They didn't talk much on the drive to the farm. Hank wondered if Molly was sorry she'd agreed to keep him. She kept her eyes on the icy road. The windshield was frosted, and she had to lean forward from time to time and wipe it with her glove. Hank rubbed his hands together and blew on them.

"One of the first things we'll have to do is get you some proper winter clothes," Molly said, still watching the road. "It's a wonder you didn't freeze to death out in that blizzard."

Hank didn't know what to say, so he didn't say anything.

Finally, because it seemed he should, he said, "Sorry about your father."

Molly sighed. "Me too," she said. Hank noticed a tear in the corner of her eye.

"And I'm sorry I ran off that time, after the fight. I was mad and I was only thinking about myself."

"You had a lot to think about," she said. She glanced at him and smiled just a little. Hank smiled, too. He felt the ice that had formed in the pit of his stomach begin to melt.

Poe was waiting for them when they got home. Molly put the kettle on, and Hank got out the mugs for tea. They spent the afternoon cleaning out the room behind the kitchen. It already had a small bed and dresser, and together they brought a bookcase and desk down from the attic.

Hank made the bed, and Molly brought in a pile of books from the living room. "Dickens," she said. "You can have them for your own."

Hank ran his hand over the gold-embossed bindings. "Really?" he said.

"Really," Molly said.

When they were finished, Molly said, "Get your coat. We're going visiting."

"Visiting?" Hank said. "Who?"

"You'll see."

They took the sleigh this time, and rode across the field. It wasn't long before Hank had figured it out. Hattie's. They were going to the Jansens'.

When they arrived, a black automobile was parked in front of the house.

"What do you suppose he's doing here?" Molly said. She looked alarmed.

"Who is it?" Hank asked.

"The doctor," said Molly. "I hope Mrs. Jansen is all right." Hank knew from listening to Emily that Mrs. Jansen had been ill for a while—after losing both of her children, one to measles, the other stillborn.

Molly hitched the horse, and Hank climbed out. He was about to knock when the door opened. "Well, look who's here," Mr. Jansen said. He ushered them into the warmth of the kitchen. "Elizabeth!" he called. "We've got company."

Elizabeth Jansen came out of a room down the hall. "Hank," she said, "and Molly. Just what the doctor ordered." She didn't look ill to Hank.

As if on cue, the doctor came out of the room. He nodded at Hank and Molly. "The girl's going to be just fine," he said. "I'll check on her in a day or two." He nodded again and let himself out.

"What happened?" Hank said. "Is it Hattie?"

"There was an accident," Mr. Jansen said. Hank thought he must have seen the look of panic on his face, because he quickly added, "She's all right. You go on ahead in. She'll be glad to see you. She's been worried about you."

Worried about me? Hank thought. He felt his ears go hot. He rubbed his hands nervously on his pant legs.

"Go on," Mr. Jansen said again. He grinned.

Hank went down the hall to the room he'd seen Mrs. Jansen and the doctor come out of.

Hattie was lying on the bed with the pillows propped up behind her. Hank was surprised to see Emily, too. He just stood there and looked at Hattie while Emily told him all about the accident. How Hattie's cat, Cloud—the one he'd seen her with the day at the claim shanty, he figured—had fallen through the ice in the cow pond while the family was away and had frozen to death.

"When they got back, Hattie went to get Cloud out and she fell through the ice herself," Emily said. "Mr. Jansen found her. She was pretty sick for a while, but she's so much better now." Emily beamed.

Hattie spoke up. "And now Emily's come to live with us! Isn't that wonderful?"

Hank nodded. It was as though his tongue were tied in a knot. He could feel himself grinning.

"Sit," Hattie said finally. "We've been so worried about you. Henry said you were missing."

Hank sat in the chair next to Hattie's bed. He shrugged. "I wasn't missing," he said. "I was at Molly's. Just nobody knew it, that's all."

Hattie laughed, and Hank blushed, realizing how silly that had sounded. "And now I'm going to be staying there," he went on. "Forever."

"I'm glad," Hattie said. "And you'll be back at school. And I'll get to see you every day." The way she said it gave Hank the feeling she'd been thinking about it—about him—for a while. His cheeks were beginning to ache with all the grinning. He could hardly wait for school, even if he did have to deal with Mr. Givens. It wouldn't seem so unbearable with Hattie there.

24

Hank pulled the covers up to his chin. He was warm and full. After their visit to the Jansens, he and Molly had come home and had supper at the kitchen table. Then they sat in the living room by the fire. Molly had talked about the funeral and about her father. She had cried, and so had Hank.

"He sounds like Mr. Olson," Hank had said.

Molly had nodded. "Why my mother put up with him, I'll never know."

"Why did you?" Hank had asked. "Why does anyone put up with a person like that?" It was a good question, Hank thought as he lay in his own bed in his own room. But right now the answer didn't seem to matter so much.

Hank wondered where his brother was, whether he would ever see him again. He hoped that someday Peter would get off the train in town and ask after him. And someone would tell him Hank was doing just fine, living out at Molly McIntire's place. He hoped Peter would appear on the horizon, a dot that kept getting bigger and bigger until his whole body took shape and Hank could recognize his long-lost brother. He hoped, but he didn't count on it.

For now, he would be happy to live with Molly and tend the birds in the barn. He would finish school, and maybe go to college. His mother had dreamed of that.

Maybe one day he would be a teacher—much better than Mr. Givens. Or an animal doctor. Or an artist. But he had lots of time to decide.

He picked up the copy of *Oliver Twist* that lay on the table next to his bed. Hattie hadn't read it yet. He'd asked. Tomorrow, after his chores, he was going to her house to read to her.

He blew out the lamp and closed his eyes. In the distance a train whistle blew. Hank smiled. For once it didn't sound lonely.